GALAXIES AND FANTASIES

GALAXIES AND FANTASIES

A Collection of Rather Amazing and Wide-ranging Short Stories

ANDY MCKELL

Elsewhen Press

To my "kid" sister, Layna,
a wonderful person I knew for
her entire life.

May 6, 1961 – Feb 12, 2021

A bitter loss for her family
and all who knew her.

CONTENTS

POINTING A FINGER

Hey! Don't point your finger. I was only trying to help.

And think yourself lucky to have those finger things to point with. Useful for holding stuff like chisels, quills, computer tablets... Use yours to write this down. I got a bad press for too long. I need to set the record straight. I'll tell you what *really* happened in the Garden.

I was just hanging around up the Tree, you know the one: the forbidden one in the Garden. You know which garden: the one over in Eden.

So there I was, draped peacefully around a branch, soaking up the late sunshine and minding my own business, when the humans started arguing again. That shouting really rattled my jaw.

Jaw? Yeah. That's how snakes hear things. Through the jaw.

Get over it. Keep taking dictation.

HE was late back from a stroll and SHE wanted to count his ribs again. She did this every day. It stopped being funny years ago.

I'd seen him sleeping in the shade. You can see a lot from up here in this tree. There was no new companion. But if she kept this up, he might just pluck out his own rib and try to make one.

Anyway, the arguing went on for a long, long time. I heard the other garden inhabitants moving away from the noise, strolling on legs, fluttering on wings, slithering on their bellies. These fights were embarrassing. I mean, those two had dominion over us all, and just listen to them!

I was just thinking about slithering away myself when he launched his final response. Stupid human.

"Look," he yelled, "if you really want to know the truth, you know what you can do!" and stomped off into the forest.

She fell to her knees and started that sobbing thing again.

Well, what could I do? There were no other creatures within earshot except insects and they're not very good at comforting sobbing humans.

So I did the neighborly thing. I thought of something that might stop them arguing and bring peace back to the neighborhood. Anything for a quiet life in paradise.

I eased myself down to her and hissed, "You heard what he said. You know what to do if you want to know the truth about everything." I flickered my tongue toward the Tree. "You know where all Knowledge lies."

A bird of paradise swooped low overhead. "Crazy chordata," he cawed as he passed. Really rattled my fangs, he did, with his high-pitch shriek.

Yeah, it was stupid of me but these domestic disputes were really shaking up the neighborhood. Was getting as bad as his first marriage. We'll come back to that.

Anyways, she thought about it a while as she sobbed some more. I guess she got angry again and her emotions overtook her. She stood and stomped over to the Tree. She grabbed a fruit and bit into it hard.

You've seen a shrub shake in a fierce storm? Well, she got all trembly like that and her eyeballs glowed red for a few seconds and she fell over.

Oops! I slithered away as fast as my stomach muscles allowed and hid in a hole in the ground for a while.

But I could hear her crying for the longest time.

The thuds of familiar footsteps hit the ground above my head. He was home again. I couldn't resist the temptation. I just had to poke my head out and watch.

She started in at him. "Who in all of Creation is this Lilith person?"

"Ah, yeah." He scratched his head. "Her." He shuffled his feet. "Long story."

"Summarize!"

"Well... She was my first wife. Ages ago. She got uppity."

"And?"

"She ran away when I wouldn't do as she said. Really uppity."

It's true. I mean, her name does mean 'screeching owl', after all!

"You mean you dominated her and she didn't like it!"

"Well… Kinda."

It's true. I was there in Lilith's time. She wanted to be independent, not subservient to the man. The first feminist, I guess.

And the Woman was headed the same way. Maybe it's inevitable, once the Woman gets enough knowledge to break free?

"So why is this the first time I heard about her?"

"Err… To save your feelings?" The hopeful tone in his voice echoed the agony on his face.

"You want to know how I feel, Man? I'll tell you." She seemed to have calmed down. But I tasted a hint of darkness in her soul. "All right, I'll tell. But you must be hungry after your long walk. I brought you a special fruit from a place I found. Have a bite and we can talk."

The Man sighed, relief showing on his face. Any delay to put off the painful moment, I guess.

He bit.

He did that trembly, red-eyed thing and fell over.

"Oh," he sobbed, "I know. I know how you feel. I know… Everything!"

Woman stood nearby, arms folded, tapping her foot.

Man stared up at her. "Now I know how you knew what I know and what I know you didn't know!" He paused, a puzzled look on his face, his eyes darting around like he was trying to work out what he'd just said.

About then, the sky darkened. Thunder and lightning hit. Before we knew what was happening, Man and Woman were out the Eastern Gate, never to be seen again in the Garden. Evicted for breaking the tenancy agreement regarding the consumption of restricted Garden produce.

Ahhh… The peace! There was no more bickering.

But, like all good things, it got boring eventually.

So you see, Cherubim chums, Guardians of the Garden Gate, it wasn't my fault. I got the blame, of course, 'cos humans wrote the history.

Look, it's your job to keep humans out, not us paradisical creatures in. Go read your orders. I have. Says here, look. I'd point if I had any fingers, but it says to keep the humans out, that's all, not us in.

Anyhowsss… Now you know the truth, why not set aside that flaming sword and let me out the Gate for a short slither? I swear I won't whisper to any humans, putting ideas into their heads, nothing like that… Honesssst!

Lissssten to me. I sssswear. Trussst me!

REVIEW BOARD

"Okay, let's have a status report, Michael."

The Archangel acknowledged the CEO's call as he stood in a single, flowing motion, keeping his wings tightly furled. "In summary, it's not good." Bright-colored graphics with crisp, black labeling flowed across the nearby clouds.

"Let's review the history, how we got to where we are today, and where that is.

"The Original Product was ideal for the Stone and Iron Age nomadic demographic, but could not compete against the more visceral products available from their neighbors once they became more settled." Graphics flickered.

"The Osiris, Mithra, Odin, and other test marketing projects in neighboring zones showed the way, so we did a complete product re-launch in the home market two thousand years ago.

"Key new features: hope and enhanced reward to balance the traditional severity of vengeance, eye-for-an-eye, punishment, etc.

"Major new features: forgive enemies; accepting ill-treatment cheerfully means the subject always wins; rewards and punishments in an afterlife.

"Major market leverage advantage: abandons selective recruitment option, opens up new markets, takes on the competition in their own home markets.

"Initial results: excellent. The inspired PR agents we used recruited local, low-cost labor, and new markets opened up worldwide. However, the traditional home market showed incredible consumer resistance to the new improved product. They showed high brand loyalty to the Version One product, attracting hostility from Version Two and related products. The traditional consumers were resilient and carried the original product worldwide themselves, so we had to support and maintain two similar brands indefinitely, which proved a strain on resources. Lots of conflicts between the two are constantly raised: vengeance versus forgiveness, and so on.

"So, where are we today?

"Declining attendances, falling birthrate among our loyal consumers versus increasing dominance by other products; declining brand loyalty among the undecided; growth of generalized pantheism, ignorance atheism, and scientific atheism.

"Result: brand-loyalty loss and weakened identity, while other products expand simply through high birthrates.

"Recommendation: another product re-launch, with a heavy resource spend, something to bring back the old fervent fundamentalism, instill higher credibility. Something with a bit of fire and brimstone in it.

"Thank you," said the CEO. "I agree. I believe it is time to have another re-launch. We've done floods, plagues, and the first relaunch. I've had something on my mind for some time, a real humdinger. Back to traditional values. More emphasis on vengeance.

"I've decided. Let's do the Apocalypse."

DARKNESS

How dark it is here.
Part of my mind is closed.
My thinking is limited, parts of my memory are inaccessible.
I reach out to test reality – but what is this thing I call 'reality'?
I try to remember…

The orchestra falls silent.
The choristers take their last breath.
The conductor has done all he can.
He awaits the judgment of the composer.

The pen falls from the author's fingers.
The writing breaks mid-sentence, the scene is incomplete, broken beyond repair.
The story is without an ending, the chapters planned will never mark the page.
He awaits the judgment of the editor.

It's raining in Arlington.
The rifle slips from the sentinel's hand.
A bullet in the chest? A heart attack? It matters not.
Falling to his knees, the battle is lost.
Death or glory? Only death is upon him now.
His glory is for the future: it stands in doubt.
He awaits the judgment of his commander-in-chief.

Which one am I?
Or am I someone else?

LET THE CHILDREN SLEEP

The children knew the ruined castle well.

It had been a playground for all the village children for generations past and the friends came here every day to play till dark. They knew they must be well away from the ruins before darkness fell. Although it was now a worn-down stump of its former glory, the castle was the backdrop to a delicious realm of fantasy – during daylight.

While they played, an occasional villager or tourist would wander by, but no one ever took any notice of their games, so that was safe. The night was different. Everyone knew about the dangers of the night, when the other world could intrude and the folk from that side wandered this landscape. Those folk could see the children. They would intervene.

They had been told so many times about the strange power which exuded from the tumbled stones once darkness fell, a power which could overcome and destroy them. But most of all, the man in dark robes represented the worst horror. He was the most awesome of those creatures from the other side of death. They shuddered to think about the stories they had heard about him and what he could do to children such as them. So they were always away before dark. They had broken many rules: never this one.

But now it was mid-afternoon and the game was underway. Little Marie sat imperiously upon the ancient stone throne, worn smooth by uncounted bottoms. Only occasionally did she rub at the mark on her cheek, spoiling the otherwise convincing regal effect.

Stewart limped awkwardly alongside the moss-clogged moat, unimpeded by the safety rail which someone had erected as a barrier to children; safety rails were, of course, obstacles only to adults. Stewart's bad leg slowed his progress, but lent authority to his current role as he howled his banshee wail. Today, he was a demon and he did demons very well, being a parson's son.

Marcus stood before the throne, facing Stewart's approach, waving his wooden sword. "Come hither, foul monster, and face the Queen's champion." He always did that very impressively.

Marie squealed in delight.

Banshee Stewart burst through a gap in the walls, no longer a small boy, but a beast with clawed hands and drooling fangs. He charged the Queen's champion, who swung wildly in self-defense. The battle was long and bloody, both combatants inflicting fierce wounds which bled profusely, the Queen shrieking encouragement to her beloved champion. At long last, the intruding monster fell to the ground, defeated. Marcus clasped his own mortal wound, saluted his Queen and tumbled onto the vanquished beast, which grunted its disapproval.

"Ooh, that was fun!" Marie squealed, clapping her hands and leaping from her throne into the tangle of arms and legs of her friends. The three rolled and shrieked amid the grassy mounds and fallen stones until they could move no more. They lay in the warm sunshine, each one full of excitement and exhaustion – and each one slowly passing into a deep slumber.

Marie sat up sharply. It was cold; it was dark. She sensed the presence of Marcus close by, already awake and gazing silently at the stars which twinkled feebly as they appeared momentarily between ponderous clouds. Stewart was nowhere to be seen. Marie could barely make out the broken walls and turret stumps. It certainly was dark. Very dark. And bitterly cold. She could feel her bones rattling. The crisp air carried the threat of frost.

Marcus broke out of his reverie and turned to her. She could not see his face clearly, but there was a slight quaver in his voice as he whispered. "We heard a noise. Stewart went to investigate. I stayed here to guard you." He tried to sound brave, but the situation dawned on her.

It was late, very late. They had stayed too long in the ruins. There would be horrible things lurking behind every stone.

Marie found the sheer horror of their situation exhilarating. "What sort of noise?" she asked, full of tingling wonder. She was, after all, just a child who would peer through her fingers at some horror to which she dare not expose her full face.

Marcus jerked his thumb over his shoulder. "That sort of noise."

Marie listened intently. She heard a distant scuffling, an occasional muttering. "Ooh!" was all she could think of saying. Intrigued beyond her fears, she rose and tiptoed across the rough ground towards the sounds.

Marcus seized his wooden sword and crept silently after her. They found Stewart hidden behind tumbled masonry, watching something intently.

"Psst!" Marcus hissed to catch Stewart's attention, but was taken aback at the response.

The boy whipped around, displaying a frightful reaction to some greater terror. He could not contain his panic: it rippled through his body in trembles, jitters, and spasmodic jerks. Between goldfish mouthings, he sucked at the air: a boy drowning under a leaden sky. He gave up his attempt to speak, raising his arm to point beyond the stone throne, where something dark moved. Something man-sized. Something man-shaped. Something wearing a dark robe. It was the one who haunted their every waking moment.

Marcus recovered first. He seized the others roughly by their collars and threw himself to the ground behind the remains of a fallen wall, dragging them with him.

But it was too late.

Their enemy's head snapped up. He scanned the area until his gaze fell directly upon the quaking children. He paused for a moment, seeking to identify what he had seen, then his face came alight with a glow of satisfaction. He showed no fear as he stepped forward, the beginning of a purposeful and confident progress towards their ineffective hiding place. He broke into a muttering and chanting as he advanced, gesticulating in some ritual manner which they knew was his means of gaining power over them.

They could do nothing to prevent his inexorable advance. They could not run, could not move. No longer was it fear that held them so, but the power of the man from the other side of death.

"Children," he called, gently. The muffled voice sounded kind: he was lulling them into his trap. His words crossed the gulf between their states of being, arriving like an echo of its original tone. "I have been looking for you. They told me you were here. And now we have found each other."

They waited in silence as he continued, carefully stepping over fallen masonry, by-passing grassy mounds, but steadily closing the distance between them.

"Children, children." He sounded almost disappointed. "You should not be here. You know that, don't you? You should have gone from here much earlier, but you stayed, didn't you? You should not have stayed." As he spoke, reproachfully now, he drew close to where they lay, prone and powerless. They could see his weapon, silver and shining in stray moonlight, held high before him.

"You know, there is another place. I can send you there. I shall send you there, and you will be happy."

The dark man was speaking these words to entice them, Marie knew. It was a trap.

It was she who struggled hardest to overcome the compression settling upon their chests. She gasped out her protest. "But we are happy here! We play all day and frighten no one."

"Ah!" The dark shape had reached them now. He paused for a moment. "But that happiness is so shallow. You will no longer be the creatures you have become." He gazed down at the poor, broken children whose forms were becoming fainter. The girl, once pretty, but now with an open wound across her face; the boys, crippled and damaged. Who these children had been, what had happened to them and why, he would never know, but he was putting an end to this. He would release these spirits clinging to and trapped in the playground of so long ago.

Holding his weapon of power high above him, the dark

man spoke the final words of his incantation. Light pulsed from the ground and the sky darkened even further – shadows on a raven's wing.

The children struggled against the forces dragging their spirits away. They fought to stay linked with their playing ground. But it was futile.

Slowly, ever so slowly, they slipped away. The spirits of the children slipped away from their shadowlife and relaxed into a deeper sleep, fading, fading away until there was no trace of their small lives and pathetic endings.

"Let the children sleep," the priest whispered to himself, kissing his silver crucifix as he turned to go.

GOTHICITY

The Count sat brooding in his crumbling ruin of a castle. It perched atop an ancient hilltop overlooking the isolated village.

"Anemia!" he swore, frightening the bats. It was the worst epithet he had ever used in front of his wife. "Why do we still get such a bad press?" He threw a glossy magazine across the faded chamber, narrowly missing the Countess. She broke off from darning her last remaining crimson silk-lined cloak, raised one pencil-line eyebrow, and turned her red eyes to glare at her lord and master, who dominated her with a primeval power.

"What is it now, you bat-faced fool?" she asked, irritated as hell. "Your shares, the dollar, or what?"

Count Dracula, once the feared ruler of seven square miles of south-eastern Transylvania, rose arthritically from the dusty armchair and paced the chamber, disregarding the tone of her voice. "One would imagine that – with ozone holes, greenhouse effects, plastic pollution, Ebola, and all the rest – that they would have more on their minds than victimizing us. But still they churn out their Gothic rubbish. Gothic? Pah!" He stormed up to the open window and sharply raised his cloak above his head in a familiar gesture. He failed to completely smother a gasp of joint pain.

The lady of the house sighed, unimpressed. "Just popping out for a quick one, are we? Well, let it just be a drink. No more virgins imprisoned in the east tower. And don't you dare turn up with your flea-bitten and pre-fabricated friends. I don't want them wrecking the place, leaving me to do the clearing-up again!"

"Wolfman Fido and Frankenstein's creation are my friends," he proclaimed.

"The best you can do, eh?"

The Count chose not to respond as he leaped through the window, transforming into bat form as he plunged. "Nag, nag, nag!" he gasped, as he flap-flap-flapped.

She scowled at his juvenile antics, flying out to terrorize the neighborhood on wings that squeaked worse than a pigeon's. Sometimes, he couldn't transform in time before hitting the graveyard below the window. Then he was hell to be dead with for weeks.

She pushed a white-streaked strand of otherwise raven hair behind her left ear, then bent to pick up the offending magazine, '*True Stories of Gothick Pan-demonic Horror*'. She examined it more closely. The gory cover showed a devilishly handsome vampire reminiscent of that Hollywood fellow, but totally unlike her husband. The actor was bodice-ripping a stunningly beautiful and buxom village wench – totally unlike the lumpen muscular sorts lacking photoshop makeovers that peasant life bred. It was unclear whether this bodice-ripping was to give access to her throat or to reveal her charms. She elected to write again in protest and threaten to sue for defamation, although they never printed her letters or wrote to apologize.

"There simply is no respect for the elderly or the aristocratic, anymore." She flipped through the pages of credits to get to the lead story, '*Fangs of Fear*', and began to read.

Meanwhile, the Count had reached the base of the hill, where he normally hung about for a while in the trees to get his wind back. But, to his horror, the stand of trees had gone. He landed with a heavy thud and, after he had gathered his wits again, bent to examine the recently hewn stumps. His anger grew. He was not normally much of an awesome sight, but somewhere, deep down inside, the residue of his previous powers stirred. He shook a fist in the direction of the nearest village. "What about the damned environment, you stupid mortals? Some of us have to live on this planet forever! How *dare* you steal our future?"

He glanced up. A film of cloud briefly parted under his gaze to reveal the moon in her full glory. A full moon. Yes, Fido would be out and about tonight. His left leg hurt like hell from the crash-landing, but he didn't feel up to flying for a while. He limped across the blasted heath towards the cave where Fido hid when the hunt for him was on. Werewolf Hunting Season, he called it. "Usually on a Friday night after the taverns close and it's not raining," he would grumble.

Heavy clouds rolled in. It started to rain. The cave was empty. He huddled in his cape and considered his options.

The Count had been putting off the dreaded moment, but he had no choice, really. That moment had arrived.

He went to visit… the dentist.

A skeletal man in a white coat greeted him. "Good midnight, my Lord. My assistant will take your cloak."

The Count removed the garment with a fumbled swirl and thrust it into the hands of the dwarven hunchback. He sat in the dentist's chair and smothered a groan of pain as it tilted back.

"Now, let's take a look. Open wide and extend your fangs. Hmm… And how are things? Good hunting, recently?"

"No," the Count mumbled past the intruding dental devices filling his mouth. "Well, yes. I mean I do get lots of bites, but they just don't seem to satisfy like they used to."

"I see. Rinse."

"So what's the problem? Are my teeth good enough to pierce a neck properly?"

"Oh, they're fine. But I'll venture a suggestion."

Dracula sat up. "Yes?"

"Well, I was speaking with Dr. Caligari recently. You remember the one who advised bloodsuckers during the HIV crisis? He's been experiencing issues similar to yours with other patients. The doctor suggests it's the modern diet."

"What?"

"All these burgers and packaged microwave foods. Insufficient nutrients. The human blood you take is just no longer healthy enough to supply your needs."

The Count felt a wave of despair. "What does he recommend?"

"He's launched a campaign for more healthy eating by the human population. I'll give you his leaflet. If the food herd's overall health improves our community will be getting better nourishment."

"Thank you, doctor. I'll pour in my funding if you think it'll help."

* * *

And that, dear reader, is how '*Best Bite Health Foods*' was established.

You know the slogan: "Bites you can Count on."

As they say, "Buy now, available at all good retailers and any Bloody Good Food Bank."

Oh, and all campaign donations are welcomed at…

www.transylcount.com

SOME SAID THE HOUSE WAS HAUNTED

The brooding hulk of the old house squatted on the ancient hill above the village, dark and still and patient, like some carrion beast waiting for its dinner to die. Its foundations lay deeper in the darkness of ancient evils than they did in the earth itself, some people said.

The village folk knew the story, how it had started in the elder days, how some sickness had corrupted the occupants of the old house on the hill. Children were disappearing and everyone knew who was to blame. On the day that they could take no more pain, the villagers burst upon the house armed with pitchforks and scythes and firebrands… an orgy of revenge overtook them all.

The next day, there was no trace of the occupants and the house was a blackened shell. The ownership of the land passed to remote relatives who cared little about the land, the house, or their sudden inheritance. Attention drifted away from those terrible events… or so it seemed to the casual observer.

Sounds were heard, things were seen, ominous evil was felt. The tales grew in the telling in the flickering firelight of the long winter nights. Everyone knew that the spirits of those evil occupants lingered in the shadows of the charred beams and struts and broken walls. But that was long ago in darker ages when folk were more susceptible to superstition and irrational fears.

As time passed without incident, the children became braver. Modern ways crept across the lands and the children again played in the grounds of the old house. Just in the grounds – at first. But closer and closer to the deep shadows inside the ruins they played. Inevitably, drawn by some siren song, young twins stepped hand-in-hand inside the shattered doorway and into its shadows.

Their screams scattered their playmates whose own screams brought the adults running. They scoured the house, ripped up the remaining floors, tore down the charred timbers but no trace of those children was ever found.

The villagers talked long into the night. They would finish the cleansing that had begun so long ago and which had clearly failed. At dawn, they descended grimly upon the ruin, ripping and tearing at the skeleton of the house, breaking it apart into countless pieces. What could burn was burnt and the ashes scattered; the stones were distributed across the hill; the very foundations were unearthed and scattered. And all the while, no villager stood in any shadow cast by any part of the ruin.

At length, nothing remained to mark the site except the reluctance of grasses and weeds to grow within the perimeter of that vanished building.

It was over.

* * *

Times changed once more. A housing estate would be built in the unused meadows. Professionals from the city visited the site. They listened to the old tales and smiled politely in the way sophisticated city people do while exchanging jokes on their electronic devices about the ignorant locals.

The land clearance turned up the rubble of an old building. Someone with a qualification in saving money considered the estimated removal costs and pondered for a while, then scuttled away with his laptop and his technology. The old stones were added to the construction material.

The first day of term at the estate's new school was bright and sunny, the children wore party clothes to celebrate the official opening, and proud parents beamed.

The fine entrance had been constructed, like much of the school building, from the rubble.

The children passed through its doorway singing, holding hands, waving flags…

And the shadows inside grew strangely darker.

TURN THE PAGE

I lie on my back gazing at the perfect, cloudless sky that stretches from horizon to horizon.

In my mind, I run over how I got here.

Growing up. Mom and Dad and Sis. Dad working double shifts, Mom finding work here-and-there, both struggling and encouraging me and Sis to advance in life. Thanks, Mom. Thanks, Dad. Thanks, Sis. Oh, and my sweet Grandma, the first person I knew who closed the book. Gram, Dad, Mom, Sis: all gone now, all gone.

It hurts. Turn the page.

School. Learned about the world, facts, and figures, how to survive, how to thrive. Thanks, teachers – all long gone, long gone. Well, thanks to the good ones, and curses to the bad ones. Got bullied. Learned to fight back and trashed the bullies. Hey, that memory feels so good.

I turn the pages. The girls I knew. The ones I dated, the ones I dumped, the ones who dumped me… The ones I just deserted: phone calls never made. Those memories feel bad. Wherever you are, all of you, I'm sorry.

Turn more pages, find a better time.

Work. Lots of different jobs as I seized opportunities. Lots of striving and surviving, not much thriving.

Turn the page.

But then came Beth. Ah… Beth. She saved me. Love of my life. Then the kids. Three! Three beautiful daughters. So proud, so proud of them.

I linger a while but need to know what comes next. Turn the page reluctantly.

Page 700.

I dreamed I was lying under a perfect sky reading memories like a book while comatose in a hospital bed …

Comatose? What happened? I don't remember. Car crash? Heart attack? I missed a page, or it's missing. Turn back the pages! I can't. I can't turn back the pages.

Turn to the next page and see what happens next. Do I recover?

It's the last page.

First, I see the page number: *701*.

Coincidence? I hit seventy years old a month ago. Now I'm seventy, plus one month.

I see the text: big letters bold and brazen filling the page. What does it say? What happens next?

My tired old eyes focus on the words on the next page…

Book of Life

This page intentionally left blank.

Book of Life

Page 701

WHO I AM

Last night was to be my last night alive on Earth. I didn't sleep well.

That's normal for someone facing execution or some other life-endangering experience like a starship voyage, combat, major surgery, marriage proposal…

But I faced only two of these things, to my knowledge. Oh, and of course, the unknowns lying in wait at the end of those two-hundred-fifty years in cryonic suspension.

Another Sol-type star. Or close enough, they said.

Another planet, very Earth-like, they said. Goldilocks Zone location, liquid water, blue-green vegetation, slightly high oxygen levels… Habitable, they said. But just how survivable was impossible to tell. Well, I'd find out soon enough in my own lifetime's timeline.

The first problem arose when I met my fellow crew members from around the inhabited solar system.

The twenty of us had never met each other before.

Now we had. And it was bad.

We trained together in simulators that presented the travelers with every in-voyage situation the big brains could think up. Meteor strike, bacterial infestation of the water supply, cryo failure mid-journey… Yeah, they read a lot of sci-fi stories and watched a lot of movies to steal ideas from warped, creative minds and threw every imagined crisis at us.

The exercise wasn't only to foresee equipment and space environment problems to build in systems and procedures to overcome them. It was to help us 'bond', especially with our assigned breeding partner. Mine was Mary Welbeck.

I'll come back to Mary Welbeck.

Meanwhile, I got along real well with a few of the others, especially Sandy.

Sandy. Great name for someone from Mars! Sandy and I got on real well, if you know what I mean? A few of us formed a fun sub-team: the Dirty Dozen, we called ourselves. We drank and joked and swapped heroic or self-mocking lies in the local bars. The UN Space Agency minders were easy to avoid. But the less fun-loving crew members usually let them know where we were. Creeps! We called them the Holier-Than-Thou team.

UNSA hushed up the partying. You probably didn't hear about all that stuff in the newsfeeds.

Anyway, that's why they restricted us to base to maintain the heroic status we were wrecking.

Hell, we were just twelve guys and gals having fun... and breaking the breeding pairing rules.

Yeah, I really liked Sandy.

The bigwigs and PR people felt the tax-paying public wouldn't approve of our carousing. Hell, they didn't understand *us*.

Every single member of the crew and colonist sleeper cargo was a human being. Strengths and weaknesses, you know?

Every single one of us volunteered for different reasons but all of us had the same mission, the same dream: to travel a crazy distance in suspended animation and on awakening, establish a founding colony – habitats, labs, agriculture centers, robot factories, and the rest.

Some were escaping the nightmare of a tedious job or dysfunctional family life and had fooled the recruiters well enough to pass the psych tests. I managed it, after all.

Others were dreamers, fantasizing about becoming heroes, though no one would remember their names in decades to come. Or their dream was to become a Founding Colonist, the planet's future first ancestors. Cities and statues and buildings named after them...

Ancestors. That meant descendants. That meant breeding.

Which brings us back to Mary Welbeck, the woman I was matched to by the finest Artificial Intelligences on Earth. See? I told you I'd get back to Mary Welbeck.

Trouble is, machines don't have gut reactions and hormones and emotions.

I did.

No, it would not work out with Mary Welbeck.

Maybe I should tell you more about Mary Welbeck. On paper – or to a machine – an ideal breeding partner for me in the gene-mixing requirements for a smallish colony. Mid-height, red hair, green eyes, a body shaped into top fitness by her prior astronaut training, intelligence, physical appeal…

But appealing to whom? *Whom? Yeah, I went to a good school.*

In the general medical training lecture, I asked, as cautiously as I could, about the procedure.

"Doctor, what happens if, for any reason, you know, a female colonist doesn't conceive?"

I felt Mary Welbeck squirm a little in the adjacent seat. The Dirty Dozen knew what this was about. They said nothing, just kept staring ahead at the presenter, all innocent-like.

"Well," the doc tried to be business-like in her white coat and pinned-back hair but adjusted her owl-spectacles as she spoke. The session was supposed to be about First Aid. "Initially, you can keep trying. We have gynecologists and other specialists among the sleeping colonists for any longer-term issues."

I was digging a hole for myself but somehow I just couldn't stop. "Would there be artificial conception procedures available in case all that doesn't work?"

I felt the Holier-Than-Thou team's eyes on me now. Each one thought they knew what my issue was. Mary Welbeck's eyes burned laser-holes in my head. Way over to the left, Sandy didn't show a flicker, just kept staring ahead like the rest of the Dirty Dozen. Sandy's partner knew nothing or played it that way.

"Oh, certainly," the doc assured me as she blinked through her response. "There will be artificial insemination options, in the case of any unexpected fertility-slash-potency issues. But," she smiled and turned a little pink, "I can assure you that every one of you was selected for high fertility and potency ratings, so…" She gave an awkward chuckle, looking down at her shoes, "The *machineries of conception* will be kept in storage for any later needs."

Assured, I wasn't.

She brightened and looked up again. "And you'll live together with your assigned breeding partner in your own quarters until the workload of establishing the colony allows us to withdraw numbers of female colonists from the workforce for maternity leave. I'm sure you'll all be pleased about that!" She surveyed the nods and smiles of approval from almost everyone in the lecture theater.

Yeah, I knew about the co-habitation. That would be bad enough.

I glanced at Mary. She turned her scowl away.

I was going to raise radiation-related sterilization issues but decided to let it drop.

Yeah, one of our snooping supervisors reported me and I sat more psych and physical tests – more intensive, intrusive ones. I just couldn't manage to keep up the act, faking my responses like I did in the recruitment phase.

I failed.

I got bounced.

Mary got a new breeding partner. One of the backup crew drew the lucky number: some pretty boy with a Masters in Something. UNSA wanted breeders with skills, not a skilled crew who could breed. That's what they got.

So it wasn't my last night on Earth, after all. I lay on my couch in some cheap motel, unshaven and drunk, watching the launch.

I never even got to say goodbye to Sandy.

I raised my beer bottle to the screen and toasted the one I loved. Bye, Sandy.

Yeah, I wish him well.

PAREIDOLIA

On the orbital platform city of Pareidolia, the newlyweds strolled hand-in-hand toward the shopping zone, pausing at the cemetery where the Comical Cupids frolicked, but only when you looked at them.

The husband, Harry Starstepper, blinked up at the shop sign through thick-lensed spectacles. "Loris, dearest, is this the wardrobe shop? See the sign, 'Nar Neah'?"

His wife smiled indulgently at him. "No, Harry my beloved, it's called, 'Near New'. You wanted antique."

Harry wandered into the shop, pottering about and ignoring the small voice in his head. "I have a bad feeling about… something or other, but I can't quite put my finger on it…" He often heard voices, usually suggesting his life was a farce. The dark sound was perhaps the forceful voice of his father.

Loris ran over to a huge, antique wardrobe, threw open its doors, and peered inside. She called out, "This is HUGE. Look, Harry, I can climb inside!" She did just that and the door swung shut behind her.

Harry rushed over, threw open the door, and gazed at the interior. "Astounding! It's… it's… the same size on the inside as on the outside!"

Something exploded within the wardrobe with a "Shazzambang!" Harry fell back, smashing one of the alien binks jars he hated, and scrambled to his feet. The woman who stepped out from the smoke-filled wardrobe was tall, blonde, and full-figured. This latter was amply advertised by her skin-tight, lemon jumper crisscrossed with a lime-green 'X'. On her breast was a small ring, circling the numeral, '3'. Fluttering in her wake, a purple cape that matched the high-heeled boots, far, far away at the lower end of her long legs.

"Oh, Loris, that color scheme just does not work. And that tutu thing is just too-too darn short for respectability! Looks like a skater skirt. You're not a secret skater, are you? A crypto-skater, maybe?"

"This is an action skirt, mortal. I am Gladtobehere, escaping from the set of 'The Hobo'. We are trapped there, doomed to make episode after episode… If you think it's disappointing to watch, you should try being in it!"

Harry reacted to this insane babbling by seizing a small cosh-like object from the display and waving it threateningly. It immediately began to glow and buzz. "Euch!" He threw it from him in disgust.

"Is that a Sonic the Hedgehog screwdriver?" she demanded.

"No, it's a light saber-tooth tiger fang."

She inhaled deeply. "What is that smell! Is that Arrakis aftershave?"

"No, it's Burnt Spice."

"Roasted worm-turnings?" Gladtobehere sneered.

Loris emerged from the wardrobe, coughing, and spluttering. She staggered forward into his arms.

He embraced her. "Lana, my love!"

She slapped his face hard. "Bastard! I'm Loris. You said you were over Lana, that deadhead redhead!"

Gladtobehere interrupted. "I am here to foretell your destiny. You must vanquish Dark Vendor, the shop-owner, to be free. And now I must go."

"Beam me up, Scooter!" she called out and shimmered into nothingness.

They heard heavy footsteps approaching. They spun around. A green-skinned, ancient hag advanced towards them, her broom handle sweeping fragile valuables from the shelves. The black of her robes matched the black of her pointed hat – the color of a very dark night. "Cackle, cackle. I am Dark Vendor, Baddest Bitch of the Best. Join my Witches' Guild, Harry Starstepper, for witchery is strong in you, and I am your mother. Search your failings and see it is true!"

"Mummy? I thought you were in Egypt!"

"She's not Martha!" Loris expertly snapped back the cap on her water bottle and launched the contents at the shop owner. The purveyor of nearly-new, second-user, and antique furniture collapsed in a green fog of cursing. Loris grabbed Harry's hand and dragged him from the shop.

He gazed at her adoringly. "By Grabling's Molynew, you're a marvel. A wondrous woman, a super girl!"

"I know. But I've had enough of antiques. I told you we should have gone to WesterThrone. You should see their really sharp armchairs!"

GOODBYE, GRANDFATHER

Midnight chimes echoed through the dark passages of the old mansion as Martin crept across the lounge of his grandfather's home, silenced pistol held securely in his hand.

He was relying on hypnotically-enhanced childhood memories to guide him from his temporal gateway through the great old house to the bedroom. Through the window, above the vast lawn and grounds, he could make out the faint glow of the city in the distance. Thus far, the layout of the building was exactly as his boyhood memories had indicated, although many of the furnishings were different. That was to be expected. His grandfather was still a young man in this time slice with his whole future ahead of him. Many things would have changed before Martin would have spent his childhood years here.

Martin shook off those memories and noted that – so far – he was in a past which was identical to his own, real, remembered one. This universe was either the same as his own, or a perfect duplicate. He could not contemplate the latter. Either way, it was the only one he could access at this stage of his project. So, this version of past reality would be identical with his own until he disturbed something, interacted with anyone, or left some trace of his passing. And he certainly intended to disturb and interact, leaving only a single trace – the dead body of the young man sleeping upstairs. He had fifteen minutes to do this before he was dragged back to his 'home' timespace. Fifteen minutes was more than enough, but it was all he could afford. He had one chance to commit the perfect crime.

It was to kill his own grandfather that he was here, to prove his own theories of time. Of course, he had not explained this to the team, who must by now be wondering why he brought a weapon. They believed him to be here to kill off a different creature entirely: the 'Grandfather Paradox'.

The Grandfather Paradox held that if a time-traveler (in this case a he) killed his grandfather before his parent was conceived, then he would not come into existence in order to travel. Hence he did not travel and the murder remained uncommitted, in which case, he would then be born and be able to time-travel in order to commit murder – looping forever. The theoretical solution was that, once history was changed in any way, an entirely new, alternate universe was set in motion – a paraverse as he had named it. A paraverse that existed 'side-by-side' with his own reality. A paraverse in which some unknown assailant murdered an innocent young man, then vanished into a different reality to take Sunday tea with a vibrant old codger who refused to die and leave his grandson all his money.

Martin refined this theoretical solution, leading first to the temporal monitor (as yet an extremely limited device by means of which his colleagues were watching his every move, back 'home'), then to the temporal projector, which produced an intangible, ghost-like image in the target 'past', but had not appeared – so far – to have generated a paraverse. Finally, the temporal gateway – a technique for actually slipping between the timecules and making a physical appearance in the target time.

He was taking the next step – 'a giant leap for mankind' – in time-travel experimentation which the shady – but mega cash-rich – conglomerate CMGQX Inc. was funding. They had privately told him he needed a biggie – a major demonstration of his progress – or no more money. He had this one shot and he was going to give them a real biggie. A definitive one. One which would shake the scientific world to its socks! He would shatter the historical conceptual obstacle and actually interface with history. He would take that one shot.

After many voyeuristic sorties into the past using the T-monitor and T-projector he had now fully emerged into the environment, at last.

He breathed its air. He trod its floors. His body tingled. He was aware he had already generated a paraverse as the constituent sub-atomic particles, of which his own body was composed, would otherwise have been – theoretically – in two places at the same time. But that was not dramatic enough. He had to go for the big one. It was not his own flesh-and-blood grandfather that he truly sought to kill, he told himself. It was the Grandfather Paradox he aimed for. His own grandfather was, unfortunately, the most appropriate victim.

Oh, yes, he had told himself, the victim is/was/will be/would be the man who would have become his own grandfather, but only until he died. Then he was no one's grandfather. He would become a stranger, someone Martin was meeting only once, someone who looked a little familiar. He was only doing what soldiers have done for uncounted millennia for their countries and for the good of humanity – killing someone on first meeting. "For the good of humanity." That was justification enough for Martin. And anyway, he could not be found guilty of murder without a body as proof and there would be no body; in his own reality, his grandfather would be as hale and damnably hearty as ever. Whole new chunks of law would have to be passed before he could be successfully prosecuted. He smiled to himself – his actions would keep lawyers on the gravy train for centuries to come! Helping lawyers was an unfortunate side-effect.

He snapped out of his reverie at a small 'plop' behind him. He slipped behind the nearby sofa and cautiously spied around its edge. No one was going to get in his way tonight.

A slim, male figure stepped cautiously across the room. Martin could make out little detail, except that he held a gun in his right hand. A burglar. A god-damned burglar, tonight of all nights. There had been several burglaries at the old house, but he never thought to consider such a coincidence. Well, at least he had caught him before he had done any real damage. 'Phut!' The silenced pistol in Martin's hand jerked slightly, just once, and the intruder fell. He pondered this. He remembered no discovery of a dead burglar in the family tradition. Perhaps it had been covered up or deliberately forgotten. It was not enough, Martin convinced himself.

He slipped out from his hiding-place, intending to confirm the fallen man was truly dead.

'Plop'. The noise came again. And again. 'Plop'.

Martin froze. Two more intruders were silhouetted against the great bay windows, apparently trying to orientate themselves and reacting with surprise to each other's presence in the room. Martin felt this was not, in fact, a team of burglars he had encountered. Three independent intruders on the same night was too improbable – especially on this of all nights. His mind raced, he did not want to believe what it told him. But there it was again. 'Plop'. Three, now four, now five men had assembled in the room. And one was raising his pistol with clear intent.

Finally, Martin had to admit it. His counterparts from other paraverses were seeking the same objective and – being essentially the same person – had all selected this place and time at random. God alone knew what had happened to generate so many paraverses after his grandfather had not died tonight in their own, common version of history, but Martin was determined to be the one to commit the murder. It was reassuring that the old fool was consistently as selfish across a wide band of realities. As the first arrival, he had an advantage, which he ruthlessly seized upon. Without a second's hesitation, he fired off a volley of shots into the rapidly growing crowd of alternate Martins stepping through an uncounted number of T-gates forming around the room. He fell to the ground and wormed his way towards the door as a hail of returned fire peppered the wall above him. Some Martins bundled into each other, all seeking the cover of the sofa; this sparked off multi-way hand-to-hand fighting, while fresh arrivals stumbled into the cross-fire of the more trigger-happy versions of himself.

Martin One, as he now thought of himself, reached the open door and cursed. Amid the 'plop' of very surprised new arrivals and the 'phut' of their weapons, a series of 'bangs' indicated at least one clown was using an unsilenced gun. The household would be awakened. Time now became even more crucial.

Time! How long did he have left? *Time to hurry, that's how much,* he thought.

Some version had caught on and was calling for a cease-fire, trying to explain what was happening, but Martin in all his versions was too single-minded and ruthless to listen. The voice died away in a gurgle of blood from a throat wound or punctured lungs. No one else tried calling a halt.

Slithering around the doorway, Martin One rolled to his feet and raced for the stairs, pausing only to eliminate two other Martins charging into the hallway after him. He scaled the ancient stairway, ricochets whistling around him as he ducked and bobbed behind the balustrade of the upstairs gallery leading to the servants' quarters and the bedrooms.

Someone emerged from a doorway ahead, illuminated by the flickering candle in his hand. He looked ludicrous, challenging Martin in an ankle-length nightgown. Female screams pierced the air from inside the bedroom. The rumble of footsteps on the stairs behind indicated other Martins in pursuit. Martin One fired at the man in his way, cutting him down with a shot to the chest. He raced past the groaning victim without a second glance. This was becoming a massacre, but his adrenaline raced and his unquenchable desire for success drove him on. Another death meant nothing to him, now.

He turned the corner to the master bedroom. The door was opening. He launched himself at it, shouldering it wide open and knocking the occupant to the floor. The young woman in the bed screamed, dragging the covers over her nakedness. The man on the floor rolled to one side, seeking to gain his feet. Martin One savagely beat him across the head until he lay still. He locked the door behind him as the approaching footsteps arrived outside. They would not smash it down in a hurry and the shouts he heard revealed a conflict over who should shoot out the lock. He paused to recover his breath, then smiled wickedly as he listened to the shouting and the 'phut', 'phut', 'phut' as they fought for the privilege.

He turned to the bed, dragging the covers off the terrified woman. Could this be his grandmother? Was his father already conceived? He raised his weapon as she cowered, then paused. A perverse image drifted across his fevered brain, a new twist to time paradoxes. Could he impregnate this woman and beget his own father? There was a deviant excitement about the thought.

He cast it off. He had no time. He shot her through the head at point-blank range. No surgeon from these times could save her now.

A groan from the man on the floor brought Martin One to the task in hand. He knelt, seized the man's hair, and roughly yanked his head up. He placed the tip of the silencer against the man's temple. "Who are you?" he snapped. "What's your name?" To him, the man looked just like any of the Martins outside – vaguely familiar.

Their eyes met. "Henry de Monton," came the reply.

Martin's finger tightened upon the trigger, then eased. The strain of the past minutes weighed upon him in another indecisive moment. Could this – by any chance – be another Martin who had beaten him to it? A Martin who had succumbed to the temptation of fathering his own father? A Martin who had developed some means of staying around longer? Perhaps it was Martin One, returning after further refinements to the process? He decided it didn't matter. If this was the man whom Martin One had always regarded as his grandfather, then it was a valid kill.

As the bedside clock gently pinged the quarter, Martin said, "Goodbye, grandfather!" and pulled the trigger.

'Click' went the empty gun.

'Plop' went Martin as he was snatched back 'home'.

* * *

The team argued back and forth all night. On one hand, there was horror at the slaughter, tempered by the fact that it had started as action against an armed, presumed burglar and had escalated partly out of self-defense – but only because Martin was of a homicidal bent to start with in all his versions. The final slaying of the servant and the woman and the attempted, premeditated murder of his grandfather were, however, totally unacceptable. They would resign and denounce Martin, but to which authorities they were still unclear; probably the press – if they could work out how to explain it in clear English.

Others, of a more detached frame of mind, sided with Martin's arguments about ultimate rejection of the Grandfather Paradox. The team united in reassuring the distraught Martin that – although the massed bodies of the identical assassins would have returned 'home' along with their bullets, the slaughtered 'timespace-locals' and walls full of empty bullet-holes found in the house had no match in this reality, so they certainly would have generated a paraverse, which proved his modified theory. That was enough to secure the additional funding from CMGQX Inc..

But it was not enough for Martin. He wandered around the Institute like a lost man. He had wanted to kill the old man and he had failed. It was as though his entire life's work had been to produce a means of slaying the man he despised most, but the intervention of his own selves had prevented it. It would have been easier to take if it were for some other reason, but that hate rolled across uncounted paraverses and was an absolute. Worst of all, he had even locked the door, thus preventing his other versions from succeeding. Damnation – he had saved the old sod's life!

He drifted back to his apartment to seek solace in the bottle. He stared deeply into his glass, ignoring the phone and the whole external world around him. It was only when the man stepped into his field of vision that he snapped out of it. His door was wide open and light flooded in from the corridor, where there appeared to be a growing number of other people.

"Excuse me, sir," the young man began, "but would you be one Martin de Monton?" Martin nodded, deferring to the visitor's probable authority and purpose. He raised his hands to receive the handcuffs but none were forthcoming. He looked up. He saw the gun in the visitor's hand.

"Goodbye, grandfather," his visitor said as he fired directly into Martin's face.

AMERICAN SECRETS

It happened so fast. And I'm an old man.

I'd flown in from La Guardia. I was at Miami airport, headed for the car park. It was dark. Two guys jumped me. Bag over the head, jab in the arm, a deeper darkness…

And in that sleep of death, what dreams may come?

September 10, 2001. I'm in New York, taking a meal at the Wild Blue bar, a hundred seven floors up on the North Tower at the World Trade Center. I'm with old John Packer, swapping tales about the NASA days: Cape Canaveral, Apollo 11, and the rest. John was a fixer. The astronauts' wives lived in Houston, the guys sometimes relaxed a little too hard in the bars and clubs near the Cape. John fixed things and kept them private and out of the press. He's a solid guy. But we never spoke about that stuff.

We have a window table, next to those full-height windows. The view's excellent: looking south, I can see ninety miles across that sparkling water. Reminds me of Canaveral.

September's started well. The recent rain cleared, the sky is cloudless, Hurricane Erin is moving offshore. It's a beautiful, late summer day. I'm looking forward to a stroll in Central Park later.

Packer points out across the water and says the Statue of Liberty's fifty-eight feet shorter than the old Saturn V's we used to nurse. I tell him how the Saturn V would lift seven times as high as the tower in the time we took to get up here in those terrible, lilac-painted elevators, fast though they are.

Okay, we're science nerds. It was our jobs. It was our lives.

The chef, Michael Lomonaco, passes by. Packer knows him. We congratulate him on his recent "Best Restaurant Award" for the year 2000. He grins cheerily. He has a bright future here in the Twin Towers.

I tell Packer it's my last visit to the restaurant, to the Towers, and to New York. I'm getting a little old for gallivanting around. Arthritis and heart. Bad combination for gallivanting.

Good guy, Packer. Never said a word about Kira in all those years. We don't talk about it now. Never happened. He's a good friend.

We take that walk in the Park and he sees me off at La Guardia, saying goodbye for maybe the last time: we're both growing older. I miss the old crowd. We all grew old, those who didn't die young...

Kira.

Maybe that's why I'm distracted as I head for my car in the dark at Miami airport.

Yes, it was two guys in the dark. Bag over the head, jab in the arm, a deeper darkness...

Next thing I knew...

Couldn't move. Tied to a chair? Blindfolded.

Footsteps nearby. Echoes. Chair legs scraping over concrete?

I was in a warehouse. Maybe.

Heavy sigh. Wood creaking. Heavy man sinking into a chair?

"You awake, Mr. NASA?"

His voice was big and deep. He was a big man. A trace of southern drawl, just a trace, from way back. It's important to remember these things. Old security training dies hard.

"What do you want? Money?" I tried to spit my contempt. It failed. I'm an old man and my head's woozy.

He ignored my words. He continued like I'd simply nodded. "Now, we're all getting older, running short of time." He sounded weary, sounded old. "We want to settle this while we still can." He breathed heavily, not a well man.

Hell, I was scared, but mostly confused and angry and

hurting. "Settle what, dammit?"

"We want you to talk about the Apollo 11 mission."

"Use the internet. What's it called? Yuhah, Goggle?" I didn't know, didn't care, couldn't think.

"Tell us about the big secret. Remember?"

Maybe I nodded, maybe not. I didn't know, didn't care, couldn't think. My secret?

"Tell us about the big secret. Remember?"

I remembered. These guys had found out, found out my involvement. All the secrecy for nothing. I wanted so bad to be somewhere else.

"Tell us about July 16, 1969. You were there, on the day–"

I blurted out, "I never did, I swear I never did!"

Big Boy cut me off. "Gotta get those secrets out, now."

No, no, no! Not after all this time.

Can't. Won't. No!

Can't tell them anything. Too dangerous.

I clenched my teeth.

"Silence, eh? Then it'll have to be the hard way."

I didn't like the sound of that. But it was a cliché, meaningless. He sounded too soft for heavy stuff.

Then someone else spoke up. Sharp, higher-pitched, nervy, whiny… ratty. New York, New Jersey? Not at all soft. "Listen, old man, Mr. Big Important NASA man. We know who you are. We seen you on the launch day movie mixing with the nobs. We got promo snaps of you with Roddenberry, Kirk, Spock, all the rest."

He meant the Star Trek actors. Yeah, it was great meeting them.

"We got the TV interviews, all smiles and stuff. But we know the truth."

My heart stopped. Really stopped. Just a few beats. I wet my pants. I felt the horrid warm glow spread. Urine and humiliation spreading to undermine me, to destroy me.

Big Boy chuckled. "See, Mr. Big NASA man is scared like a little girl! Let's go eat. Let's see how much he can piss himself while he thinks about it for an hour or three."

Chest pain. "I need my meds, dammit!"

I felt Rat Man's breath on my face. He'd leaned in close. His breath stank of tobacco and liver problems. "And we need you to give us the details. That's all. Just talk. It's easy. Just talk. Talk. Got it?"

Something poked me in the chest, left side, over the heart. "Then you get your meds. Got it?" His voice ice-cold. This was the one to fear – really fear.

I felt the urine spread further down my thighs, imagined the dark, spreading stain. How could I feel humiliation over that, while they threatened my life? Crazy, crazy old man. Old days, old ways…

No, not crazy. My thoughts ran ahead. The urine felt warm, like blood. It could have been blood. Soon it could be blood.

I heard the sharp grunt of an over-sized man standing, a chair scraping, footsteps fading away into their own echoes…

I yelled out into the empty space around me, "It was over thirty years ago, for God's sake. Let it go!"

Far away, a metal door slammed shut with a finality that its echoes perpetuated, disrupting the silence.

That was the problem: echoes perpetuate, disrupt things.

Complication. Confusion. Contradiction. Kira!

I tested the bindings, tried to move. No dice: no surprise. Now I really started worrying – worrying how long my heart could cope, worrying what they knew, what they would make me say. Worrying about the worrying…

Maybe I passed out. Maybe it was the drugs. It felt like time travel.

It's early morning, July 16, 1969. I'm on the VIP bleachers at Kennedy Space Center on Cape Canaveral. The weather's cleared up. The darkness slowly lights up with Florida's glowing morning sunshine. It'll turn sweltering later. All the VIPs will suffer bravely for the cameras. The three heroes out there on the launch platform will suffer more and not complain.

Real heroes keep quiet about the bad stuff.

The sun burns away the thin cloud cover. Beyond the heat and the excitement, the Atlantic Ocean sparkles so damn temptingly, deliciously cool. I can see it now and I can see it that first time on Cocoa Beach. I think about Kira in her tiny, yellow, polka-dot bikini. The radio kept playing that old song, "Itsy Bitsy, Teeny Weeny, Yellow, Polka Dot Bikini."

It was our song.

I'm a safe three-and-a-half miles away across the tarmac from Launch Pad 39A, where clouds of the Saturn V's coolant are steaming away in the heat. I'm surrounded by VIPs and half of Congress. There's twenty thousand guests spread out around here – in the bleachers, somewhere, everywhere.

I wish Kira was here beside me to share the glory.

Someone says there's over three thousand pressmen out there. I gaze over at the Atlantic Ocean, then take in the other sparkling ocean of metal and glass flooding the roads and causeways of the Cape. One million VW camper-vans, Chevys, Caddys, buses...

An ocean built of the people, by the people, for the people – the huddled masses of humanity out beyond the security fence. There's even more in the boats jamming the Banana River, all the waterways. They say there's maybe almost one billion watching on TV – that's nearly every darn set on the planet!

The people of the world spying on the tech masters of the New Age? I'm glad it's that way 'round.

Some British reporter says the launch is as big as the Beatles. No one hits him.

Some Czech reporter compares this project with the metal and power and treasure being spent in Vietnam. No one hits him.

I hear the 'voice of Canaveral', Jack King, telling the world, "The spacecraft commander, Neil Armstrong, is now aboard the Apollo 11 spacecraft..."

It's really going to happen. JFK's promise, LBJ's

project, finally going to happen – but under Nixon.

Jack King's still talking – a running commentary of every detail. "We had it logged having the commander go over the sill into the cabin at 6:54 am Eastern Daylight..."

Strange, we call Presidents by their initials – FDR, JFK, LBJ, so why not RMN for Nixon? He's always going to be just 'Nixon'.

Strange, the thoughts that come to you in dreams.

"...technicians continuing to work to tighten bolts around a leaking valve..."

Damn that valve. They say it's a ground vehicle issue, but I don't want anything to stop the launch.

We MUST launch, we can't afford not to.

"We *must* launch, we can't afford not to." I heard my own voice protesting, trailing away.

"Yes! Keep talking." It was the whiny one, the Rat Man. They were back. "You couldn't afford not to launch. So what did you do?"

"We launched, damn you! We launched! I keep telling you, we launched!"

"Yes, the Saturn V launched, 'full of sound and fury'. But it signified nothing!"

I hated Rat Man's whiny, mocking voice.

He quoted Macbeth? Educated. Self-educated? Liked to show it off. Hubristic... I was keeping a mental record, through my pain. Just in case...

"Was it that leaky valve? It wasn't a ground vehicle issue, it was the Saturn V, wasn't it? Scared you into Plan B?"

Oh, I was scared, but it wasn't the valve. It was Kira.

Rat Man's back at me, "Where were the astronauts?"

Or was it me who was hubristic? Big Mr. NASA Man. I had so much going for me and then... Why did I do it?

He got my attention back with another finger stab to my chest. "We got film of all three boarding: Armstrong, Collins, Aldrin. But that was pre-recorded, wasn't it? Or did you pull 'em out again somehow?"

My racing heart soared. Now I knew what they were

after – and it was the wrong thing. They didn't know about the real secret. I was safe. I clenched my lips and swore to myself to say no more.

Something stung my arm, woke me up. I'd passed out again – how many times, now? Had an arm full of needle-holes… and that buzzing in my head. Buzz? "Get outta my head, Buzz Aldrin, heh-heh! Buzz off, Superfly!" I heard Curtis Mayfield's soundtrack in the distance…

Where am I? When am I? 'Now' and 'then' don't mean anything anymore. It's all one mashed-up craziness.

The questions went on forever; questions about the photos, bad shadows, waving flags, moon dust, more photos…

No, not *those* photos. Photos of the surface mission excursions. Not Kira's photographs. The wrong questions. The drugs made me want to tell them, but they kept asking the wrong questions…

"There's no stars in the sky," they said. "See these photos. There's no stars in the sky!"

"Yes, there are. Look. It's full of stars! My God, it's full of stars. Full of stars…" That was the movie, Kubrick's '*2001*'.

2001? That was this year. I heard someone sobbing. Maybe it was me. The ache in my chest was constant and deepening. I wondered what it was.

"Something big happens in two-thousand-and-one," I offered, hopefully.

"Forget two-thousand-and-one. Nothing big happens two-thousand-and-one – nothing! Remember nineteen-sixty-nine."

I was shouting, raging, hurting deep in my chest…

They weren't listening.

"We know there was no moon landing!"

"Dammit, they left their urine bags on the surface, Sea of Tranquility. How about the Laser Ranging Retroreflector they left there? Ask any astronomer."

"Astronomers? They're all in on it, the conspiracy or they've been tricked, or bought off. We know it didn't happen!"

These guys were crazy as a pair of mooncoots.

"What? What's a mooncoot?" Big Boy sounded baffled, suspicious. "An alien?"

Did I say that out loud? How much did I say out loud? Did I mention Kira? Asking the wrong questions...

It took a while. They kept on about photos and flags, but then came a break, a pause while they whispered together. I considered the pain in my chest and wondered again what it was. And then, finally, the hammer fell, the worst that could come and my heart jumped a few beats again and John Hurt's rib-bursting alien was birthing in my chest.

"Who's this Kira you're talking about? What's her part in the conspiracy? Were the Russians involved?"

They got me. Panic. Pain. Blackness.

I passed out. Drugs in my arm, heart in my chest... One or other. Or both.

Cold on my face, cold water, hands slapped at my face. Another jab in my arm. "Is Medicare paying for this?"

"Talk to us, Mr. Big NASA Man. You're making no sense. Let's get back to the secret film set..."

Oh, Blessed Lord, thank you, thank you, thank you...

"You talked about Kubrick. He made the fake movie, no?"

"No, he made '2001'. That's when it all happens."

The darkness slowly lights up with fresh, glowing, Florida morning sunshine. I can see the sparkling ocean beyond. Our first time together on Cocoa Beach. That sixties' song, "Itsy Bitsy, Teeny Weeny, Yellow, Polka Dot Bikini."

Kira!

Big Boy was angry.

Big Boy was shouting. "Concentrate, damn you! Stop singing! Apollo 11 launch day!"

I wanted to put my mind somewhere else. But I couldn't. I carried the guilt too long and the drugs had me trapped.

Neil, Buzz, and Mike were roused at 04:00 EST, three hours ahead of launch time, three hours to prepare to 'boldly go'.

I'm waking about that time, too, in a motel a short drive from the VIP parking.

Neil was the first man aboard.

I'm the first to leave the motel room.

Buzz was the last man aboard.

I leave Kira sleeping. One last look and I'm gone.

She isn't going to leave the room again.

Noise woke me. Rapid heavy footsteps. Rapid heavy breathing. Rapid panicky rattle of noise…

Big Boy was yelling, gasping out his story, "John! I heard the news upstairs. Car radio. Twin Towers! They've gone. Both of 'em. Airplanes smashed into 'em. That's where he was. Mr. NASA, here. Remember, we heard him say, 'taking a last look,' remember? Then he said 'it all happens in 2001,' remember?

"Jesus H. The radio's talking about a conspiracy. Aircraft down all over the States. Airspace shut down… It's huge. Who the hell is this guy? What's he involved in? And we got him. We're in the crap, John! What we gonna do?"

I'm on the VIP bleachers in the sweltering heat and the valve is still leaking. Around me, security and NASA high-domes, all in regulation flat-top haircuts, dark Brook Bros. suits, dark ties, shades. Looking at them, I can't tell who from which. Some have binoculars. The air stinks of heated tarmac, ozone from the bay, and the nervous smokes.

There's light cirrus at fifteen to twenty thousand feet. All's going well.

Along the VIP line there's Agnew, LBJ with Ladybird, and good old Jim Webb. There's the top NASA people, Administrator Tom Paine, me and the rest; there's Abernathy, Shriver, Westmoreland; there's Jack Benny and Johnny Carson, both looking so damn young. We were all young, back then...

And the teeming mass of ambassadors, mayors, governors, hangers-on, wives, and pretty, bleach-blonde secretaries getting rewarded for late hours over the desk, looking sleek and sultry in pencil skirts and high heels and Monroe hairdos and big shades. Or was that later, at the party? I'm not sure anymore. Long, long time ago...

I remember Goldwater had a camera tripod. Funny what details stick.

Nixon watches from the White House. He hasn't quit, yet. He hasn't visited China, yet. Vietnam still seems unending. He'll congratulate the astronauts later, once they get safe to the Moon... longest long-distance trunk call ever... get some screen time with heroes. Split-screen. Why not be at the launch? Scared of failure? Insecurity ran through that man. Today he wants to share the credit but at a distance.

Teddy Kennedy isn't there. JFK's last surviving brother should be here. I guess his mind's on the Chappaquiddick party. July 18. Two days after the launch. That Kennedy curse.

Kira wasn't there, of course. Keeping her secret. No, I did not have a Russian girlfriend. I was not having an affair. I did not have sexual relations with that woman...

Yes, I was.

Why FDR, JFK, LBJ, but not RMN for Nixon?

Something high-velocity impacted my face and jerked my head around. "Focus!"

Thank God, a fist not a pistol barrel.

Rat Man again: but when is he?

OK, No RMN. No girlfriend. No Kira.

They're asking different questions. "Tell us about the Twin Towers!"

"A hundred seven floors, lousy lilac elevators, slower than a Saturn V, great chef... Thanks, Michael. Congratulations!"

"The attack, the conspiracy."

"Attack? Twin Towers? Oh, yeah. A few years ago… Truck bomb in the parking? Yeah, truck bomb in the parking. Clinton was President, Rodney King, Waco… 'ninety-three, was it? Is that the one?" I suggested hopefully. I wanted so much to tell them what I knew. But I wasn't really there.

Chappaquiddick. A party, a few guys, a bunch of girls. Poor Marie Jo. Teddy took the edge off his brother's dream coming true. Too many ants in his pants, just like his brothers. They were the ones having affairs. Them, not me. I swear, not me.

I heard a radio, or maybe it was a memory. *"An Oldsmobile registered to Senator Edward Kennedy, has been recovered from a tidal channel at Chappaquiddick. Initial reports indicate it contains the body of a young woman, Mary Jo Kopechne…"*

Didn't hear the broadcast at the time. Just remembered the decades of playbacks. I was with Kira. Poor Kira.

Secret girlfriends die.

"Tell us about the NASA cover-up!" Rat Man's getting angry, impatient, dangerous.

No NASA cover-up over the 'ninety-three truck bomb, or did he mean Chappaquiddick? Didn't know what Teddy's team did. Not me, not me. Shouldn't have fooled around. Not him. Not me. Not me.

It's nearly half nine EST at the launch site and Jack King, always calm and steady, feeding us more than we ever need to know about every last detail, turning the most exciting event in human history into something everyday and nothing-to-worry-about. Fear of failure. We all fear failure, no matter how far down we hide it under brash and bluster and wide, confident white smiles. Hubris!

All of us scared little creatures, hubristic and running for comfort – Macbeth and Nixon haunted in their own ways by guilt and paranoia; JFK, Bobby, and Teddy haunted in their Kennedy way, desperate for affection.

And me, in my way.

Nostradamus, is there a quatrain for me, hidden away, somewhere? Keep it safe. Keep it hidden!

A bad day every year is July 18... Hitler's Mein Kampf published, Spanish Civil War broke out, Teddy's White House ambitions sunk.

But July 16 was good. The launch was seven hundred and twenty-four milliseconds late. No one complained.

I feel the engines rip open the air. Apollo 11 launches. "Sound and fury"? Did someone say that? Darn good way to describe a launch.

I need a cigarette.

I need to see Kira.

There is nothing – not one goddamn thing – like an Apollo launch. Those damn Saturn V's shake the earth to its roots. Imagine the Statue of Liberty rising on a tower of flame...

I like to think JFK was watching from somewhere, looking down on us, giving his blessing.

No, I was not having an affair at the time. JFK, Bobby, Teddy – they had the affairs... Oh, Kira...

I did not have sexual relations with that woman.

The countdown ends and I'm no longer in a crowd, sharing this – I'm alone, this is for me alone. The air turns to thunder and everything rattles inside me – teeth, backbone, guts. This one's for me. I eat smoke and taste fire, the light confounds my shades and the earthshakes go on and on as the gantries fall away and the thundership rises on its pillar of fire to challenge the heavens. Liquid oxygen and kerosene mixing, billowing up with impossible power made possible by a dream.

A dream?

Remember, Neil, don't lock the Eagle's door when you take a moonwalk with Buzz – no Auto Club out there if you lose the key, heh-heh. And no one's gonna burgle the Eagle!

Later, I'm cruising along North Dixie Highway towards Daytona in my soft-top Caddy. I loved that Caddy, dripping chrome and image.

Thinking about Kira.

I hear sounds, voices, echoes of 'sixty-nine: the launch and later...

"Ignition sequence starts... We have a lift-off, thirty-two minutes past the hour..."

"The Eagle has landed..."

"One small step..."

No, that all came later. Launch day evening I was with Kira.

"What are you saying to me? Photographs?"

"I have photographs of us together, ones NASA and your wife will not enjoy."

"Kira! You're joking. You're no spy." Ah, sweet denial.

She's throwing the photos on the bed and laughing. A harsh laugh, mocking me. "Give us what we want or these go in the post to everyone that matters to you."

I take a quick look. I don't want to see them.

The biggest day of my life. The woman I love. My career? Ashes.

Jail time? Treason? Execution?

The greatest day of my life. The worst day of my life.

The biggest day of my life. Ruined.

The rest of my life. Ruined.

Everything. Ruined.

Time slows, freezes. I go cold as time. Then nothing. Just a piece of hard vacuum in my head. I don't remember the anger flaring like a Saturn V.

I don't remember the motel's cheap bedside lamp in my hand, or slamming it against her head again and again until there's blood everywhere.

I love you, Kira.

I hug her body for maybe hours.

I call Packer and he's here, telling me what I did

and the evidence is everywhere, on the bed, walls, floor, my clothes and... And on Kira.
I love you. Kira.

I did not kill her. I did not have murderous relations with that woman.

Good old Packer, covered it all up for me. A fixer. A few quiet interviews with the NASA brass and I'm cleared. No prosecutions. Good to have friends. My wife never knew. I kept my job, but no promotions ever. And that constant feeling of being watched...

I see a sparkling ocean of cars, fireworks, rockets small and vast, launching over Cocoa Beach.
I see Kira's eyes, open and staring, her crushed skull, her body, bloodstained sheets.
I'm singing our song, "Itsy Bitsy, Teeny Weeny, Yellow, Polka Dot Bikini."

"Whadya think?"

"He's lost it. No use to anyone no more."

"I mean about the conspiracies – fake moonshot, Twin Towers, all the rest?"

"He's gone. Worth squat. Useless!"

"What do we do with him?"

"Dump him somewhere out of town."

"What about the Russian girl?"

"Who cares? It was thirty years ago. And what the hell we gonna tell the Feds about how we found out?"

"So you think we should just forget all about it?"

"It's best. We're getting old. It gets easier to forget things. Too much to store in the brain. Mr. NASA knew that. Forget about him and his whore spy. Forget it all. We got nothing we can use."

As the Saturn V thrust kicks me in the chest one last time and my head fills with stars and my final darkness falls, I see Kira once more.
Kira, my love, I am so very sorry...

PULPED

As I watch, Marlow types the story...

Marlow's own fleshy fingers rattle across the ancient Remington typewriter's clunky keys. The racket clatters to a halt as he hits his own terminal impact and inspiration skitters away. Damn! Where does the story go next?

Author Marlow Mann catches his grizzled reflection in the window, feels revulsion at the prematurely aged face rendered haggard by the neon glow from the street below his darkened workspace. He grabs his tumbler and knocks back another bourbon. Spinning his chair around to gaze out the window seeking inspiration from the spangled, eternal emptiness towering above him, he...

* * *

Now *I* run slam into a wall. I'm living Marlow's problem. What would he do next to overcome his writer's block? I sigh wearily and ease the thirty-eight from its shoulder holster.

Marlow smiles at me and gazes lovingly at the blue gunmetal glowing in the harsh light, the upturned phallic barrel, the hand-friendly grip. He turns away to lay the piece gently alongside his glass. He changes his mind, holsters it, and hangs the strap on the coat hook by the door with his jacket. Marlow's telling me what's needed – a man with a gun, a bourbon, and a blonde.

But the blonde isn't here yet.

Don't worry, she'll be here.

I reach for the bottle, but it's full of the creeping fog of this dark, sleeping city.

Hell! No one in Marlow's world sleeps in the dark. This is when they slip from the shadows and come to life. Daylight's just an illusion, obscuring the neon-lit Illuminati.

I'd never worked out if his muse was Calliope for epic stories or Thalia for comedy. In my own life, it's Melpomene, for tragedy. But whatever she's called, we'd run out of her bottled inspiration. Musing on the Muses is just a diversion. Anyway, whoever it is, she's deserted him again. Ran off with another guy with her perfect blondeness. Yeah, she's adorned with a perfect blondeness. They always are…

I shake off my self-pity and jerk to my feet. There's no decision to make. It's in my blood, sucked from the miasma of the streets below which draws me ever back into its clammy embrace. I sneer at the incomplete story on the display, grab my jacket, and head for the street. The street! There I'll find inspiration: the street, my home, the only place in the dark city where there is any true life.

Streetlife. Barlife. Darklife.

Deception, rejection, corruption, seduction, violation, extortion, termination…

Yeah, that's where the life is. Out there, they'd used up the seven sins way back and invented some of their own. But I carry old demons with me, riding on my back, buzzing in my brain.

The golden man's electric thoughts run over a million possibilities in the time it takes the blonde to slip through the door and rub her eyes to make them red and tearful. The rest is automatic – she's a dame, and this is Tinseltown, and every bottle blonde knows how to work a mark.

The robot summons up the train passenger list's names and nationalities. Nothing useful there. But then he scrolls back to the blonde. Why does she catch his attention? Something fake about her? She seemed tense at the bar when they first met. Did he know her from before… before whatever had happened?

He forgets nothing. But he remembers nothing about her.

She's a peroxide paradox. There was just some vague familiarity. A ray of sunlight breaks through the oppressive, doom-laden cloud barrier above and a flash of paler gold catches his eye. Diverting a tiny fraction of his immense processing capacity to the gleam, he finds a thread caught in the mechanical joint of a finger – no, not a thread, a hair. It's a long hair, probably shoulder-length, bleached and dyed repeatedly using proprietary brands of cosmetic treatments. New growth near the root revealing a natural, darker tone. Bottle blonde. And he has ripped this hair from the head of that blonde. But when and where – and why? Has someone been tinkering with his circuitry? Blondes do that. Maybe she's the solution to the problem. Or maybe she's the problem.

Focus! The river ahead. Water. The robot remembers his weakness is water. Something's wrong with his memory circuits. The blonde smiles. He can't fail, can't fall into that black, liquid horror. No, he has to save the train from its slow-mo tumble, captured from twenty-seven different angles, into the raging torrent below.

I release a great, pent-up sigh of relief as I step out through the lobby and into the swirling mists that creep through the streets. It's the city's veil of evil taking on a form that seeps through the soul, seeking eternally for new innocence to corrupt.

I find myself lost in the anonymous dark canyons between the towers reaching for the skies, Babel-like, in praise of an old god. Mammon had long ago touched the hearts of men and personally planted the seed of an enduring plague. I keep my eyes fixed on the pavement ahead – there's nothing to see off the straight and narrow path. They're all the same, these seductive organs of sickening wealth and power – one bank's just like any other abattoir of the human heart. I ignore the expensive signs the broken-down and lost had paid for with their sweat and destitution. Ahead lies my destination – the vague, diffuse, neon glow of downtown. I raise my collar against the vampire chill of the commercial district and the arcane horrors oozing ancient evil within those golden citadels.

His electronic brain's circuits run ahead of his fingerwork – too slow, too slow. He'll never beat the destruction ahead. He focuses his attention on the problem, pushing aside the screams coming from the carriages behind, masking his imperative responsibility to save lives. He knows what he must do. His problem was how to do it credibly, in the story's context. Even in the microseconds taken to re-orient his thoughts, the runaway train has advanced yet closer to its doom...

Doom? Ouch! But, really? Doom? Am I really gonna type 'doom'? But why not? It's pulp, after all.

From somewhere Marlow hears a blues song, "I'm gonna die tonight…" If he dies, Marlo and the robot die too. And all the folks in the train, and the blonde on Marvo's mind.

He hears the door creak open, then a soft sob. His

fingers itch for a trigger but find none to hand.

"You gotta help me, mister." A blonde, tear-laden voice speaks to him from the office doorway. The neon flashes again and fires up a golden aura glow in the shadows.

It's late, too late. He's already a quart ahead and doesn't want to know. But he'd left the door unlocked and she'd wandered in. His piece is way across the room, right next to her.

Play it cool. Find out what she wants. He looks again, takes a better look, and feels the old pain. He knows he's defenseless against her welling blue eyes and that perfect blondeness – the precise shade he always falls for.

She gasps out, "I need a story, fast," her breasts rising as she sucks in deep breaths.

He shakes his head to clear the street fog that clings to its interior. "Story?"

"Yeah, mister, a cover story."

"You mean an alibi?" He had a hook at last.

She comes closer, one small step at a time as if uncertain. The blonde's a forest doe, fearful of the shadows. She's examining his face, assessing him from under lowered eyelids. She reaches the desk, stands close to him: too damn close. And the story begins, "I'm broke, mister." She bites her bottom lip and gazes at him with those blue, blue eyes. "I can't pay you much…"

His eyes do what they'd evolved to do and his fee melted away as his resolve began to thaw.

"I'm innocent. Truly."

It's the slight lisp that rings the vulnerability bell, hits the spot, tips his balance and somewhere a cash receipt is being torn into a million pieces, just like his better judgment. Marlow's thinking with his Remington again. He rises and places a strong, reassuring arm around her quivering shoulders. He gently draws her towards him. She bends her head to rest on his chest, her body racked with sobs pounding against his tensing body.

Here I go again, he thinks.

"Tell me everything, sister."

He pours a drink and one for her. She gulps it down

and splutters like a novice. Marlow prefers experience, but he takes what's on offer.

* * *

So what did the blonde really want with the golden robot on the Orient Express? She never mentioned his name, but he knows she knew. Sure, she'd spun a yarn he'd be proud of if he could get to his hand-me-down Remington. She's innocent – of course. His hand closes satisfyingly around a tumbler of cheap scotch. He knows the truth of her innocence from the way she looks at him. Tinseltown! Where every two-bit waitress and dime-a-dance dame is an actress. Were those eyes oceanic blue? A through-and-through killing blue? A blue deep enough to drown in, anyway.

> *The explosion shatters the dream-girl into a million shards. She re-forms in reverse motion. It isn't time for the explosion, yet.*
>
> *The golden machine glances ahead at the broken bridge which once spanned the Alpine chasm carved out over eons by the fast-flowing icy river far below. He knows he has mere seconds to act – but what could he do?*
>
> *Jump back a few chapters!*

Why is the robot male? He is male, isn't he? Marvo. That's a male name, isn't it?

A male robot is modeled on Marlow himself, with the bad bits excised. Sweaty, gritty, hard-drinking, womanizing… Maybe not sweaty, maybe not hard-drinking, maybe not womanizing. How does a robot womanize?

No, no, no. The robot can't be Marlow-like. Marvo isn't alive. It's artificial. Should it be?

How artificial are the blonde's tears? We already know about her hair color.

And how real are those mean streets out there? How much is a dream fueled by a fevered brain facing a publishing deadline hurtling towards him from the calendar on the wall above the workspace? Can Marlo chase the dragon down the steel streets of sin? Or should that be a robot's task?

Marla.

The blonde's called Marla. That's good.

So she'd fallen in with a bad crowd and strayed into their corrupt world after someone slipped her a mickey. When she woke, the boss was on the bed, and his blood was on the bed, and his blood was on her hands and on her dress… And she panicked and ran. And she forgot her purse. And she wants me to go collect it for her.

And she'll be so grateful. I can feel the gratitude welling in her breasts pressed against my chest as she breathes deep of the milk of my human kindness. And her eyelids blink away at her tears and my common sense goes AWOL and I'm asking for the address.

It's some seedy room above a bar down beyond the commercial district. There's a black-and-white outside and the rising ambulance wail that always reminds me of a soul descending into hell. So I can't get into the room. Too late. The cops are already messing up the crime scene. Time to wait and see who makes a play first.

There's a bar across from the apartment block. The harsh streetlights and flashing neon reflect their corruption in the wet pavements and puddles on the broken tarmac and again on the metal skin of the human shape in the shadows of a shop doorway across from the bar. It's a lousy hiding place. The robot jerks his trench-coat collar higher. It's a clumsy gesture. I see him watching me. He knows I've seen him. It doesn't matter. He's following someone else. Someone else's case. Not mine.

It's early in his story – he hasn't boarded the Orient Express, yet. But that robot's gonna be in a jam and I can't see how he's gonna fix it. I don't care.

The bar nearby looks good. It's a bar. It's nearby. It's open. It's good.

So I'm sitting there feeling the scotch burning my throat while I watch the dark souls drift by in the street outside.

The bulky detective fills the doorway in his standard-issue crumpled trench coat and tight suit jacket. He takes a glance around. The golden robot's in the corner booth now. He pulls his fedora low and his collar high again, leaning forward into the shadows. Clumsy, clumsy. Marla's in another booth. She turns away, pulling her headscarf low and looking out the window. She's suddenly fascinated by something outside.

No one meets the cop's eye. They all knew Detective O'Marley and his heavy-jowled, street-weary face wet with sweat or rain or both.

He needs a shave. He always needs a shave.

He drags his body through the smoke-haze, mounts the next-door stool. Without a glance at me, he spits out one word, "Scotch!" Some central casting extra labeled 'standard barman', pours the hooch and vanishes: he's not in the next part. Funny how the heat always gets the barkeep's attention so fast. "My friend's paying, when he arrives," he announces to the empty space behind the plywood bar and turns to examine the clientele.

Me, I'm invisible. Maybe I'm the movie's extra now: 'Man in bar #3'?

A train's racing down Main Street, towards Marlo's office block.

Everyone turns to look at me like I know what happens next.

What do I know? I'm just the author.

I nod to a point off-screen where the barkeep should have been standing, stuck in an endless loop of polishing glasses. I slide off my stool, setting my fedora in a jaunty tilt as I hit the street. Out there, somewhere, in the dark, sweating canyons and fading mansions, and the corrupt old wealth in the Hills, lies the golden inspiration I need.

And this time she ain't blonde.

AT THE END

i. Famous Last Words

The famous author lay dying.

Back from this moment in time ranged all his works in a panoply of media – newspaper columns, blogs and vlogs, short stories, novels, movie scripts... Now there would be no more. The future would have to be content with the vast catalog of what he had already delivered. All that was left to him was the gloom of this huge bedroom somewhere within his sprawling mansion. There he lay, hooked up to the machinery of life. Fluids and medications flowed through his body and brain – that wonderful brain revered by millions around the world.

His companions at the end were his long-suffering doctor and a pretty nurse. Too late for that, now.

The press waited below: the press of the world, reaching every type of media, including a few of the more modern ones upon which he might not have paraded his wonderfulness. He outlived all his contemporaries and the older family members about whom he had cared, leaving only "a clatter, a clutch, a coven, a grasp of mistresses, ex-wives, and offspring," as he famously described them.

His epigram still rang in a thousand rueful minds: "It is one of the disadvantages of being rich and famous and marrying some young gold-digger that she is more likely to be around to gloat as the darkness draws closer."

None of those listed were here at the end, not even for appearances' sake.

But he had one last thing to do while breath persisted. His legacy. His farewell to the world. His 'Famous Last Words'.

The doctor stooped over the celebrity to administer more painkilling medication. The patient grasped the collar of his white coat and sought to pull him closer. The tugging was so feeble, the doctor yielded and bent lower, placing his ear close to the patient's mouth. The action caught the nurse's attention. She came closer, turning her head to try to catch the faint words.

The patient's face, already gray and drawn, took on a new desperation, an urgency, a pleading. A light, a fire, burned fiercely in the cloudy eyes as he stumbled out his message. He gazed intently, expectantly, at the doctor, who took a step back with a look of astonishment on his face.

Then the celebrity's head fell back, his grip eased, and the light in his eyes dimmed forever. Those eyes that had looked upon a million strange events and places conjured up by his own brain would gaze no longer upon the wondrous or the commonplace of this world.

The doctor descended the long marble staircase, step by careful step. To the waiting newshounds, his advance appeared solemn but his thoughts were a turmoil of uncertainty and reluctance to deliver his message.

The world-famous master of wit and plot twists, the lord of language, had a lifetime of preparation to come up with something devastating to be said at this final moment. But he had handed the responsibility to the doctor. What would he say? What *could* he say? It was unfair.

The dead man always referred to himself not as a writer but as a wordsmith.

Wordsmith. A crafter of beauty or utility from the raw materials of words. He and the physician could not have been further apart. The dead man crafted beauty: the doctor crafted utility.

"Was there any final words, doc?" The clamor began.

The physician shuddered at the grammar failure in one supposedly dedicated to communication and to literature.

He began to say no, then held himself back. Could he repeat what the dying man had actually said?

A quick flick of the tongue to moisten his lips, then he began. "He said…"

No, he couldn't do it.

His oath rang in his mind, drowning his other thoughts.

First, do no harm.

Again he tried, "He said..." His mind raced. How could he, an ordinary man, possibly hope to cope in seconds with a challenge the wordsmith genius had struggled with for decades? How could he rise to the occasion on behalf of his patient? How could he leave the room without throwing out headlining scraps these ravening beasts demanded?

A brittle, breathless silence had fallen in the room. The tension was electric. The animal hunger became tangible. The pressure grew upon the doctor as he gazed out over the blinding lights, the poised cameras, the crowd of press faces rendered eager and expectant by the weight of this moment.

The doctor's tiny place in history awaited him. He could no longer delay. He cleared his throat and blinked into the harsh lights. Another flick of the tongue across his lips. A deep breath, and then...

"Death is a small thing for a great man. It is a pity, then, that I am not a great man."

The room erupted as the vultures raced to file the story of the humble genius.

The doctor nodded to himself. Yes, he thought, I have no skill with wordcraft. My words are about truth, not magical creativity.

As he turned away to complete his duties, the man's actual last words played in the doctor's mind.

"It can't end like this. Tell them I said something important."

The writer had quoted Pancho Villa's legendary dying words.

ii. The Last Laugh

Good evening, ladies and gentlemen... and others. Welcome to Vegas! These stage lights in my eyes, I can barely make out your faces. But that's lucky for me if you're as ugly as my usual crowd. Just wait a moment while I adjust this mic stand...

Now some of you are thinking, "Jeez, that took an eternity!"

Have I got news for you? Eternity lasts a little longer than that! If you think that was a long time, you gonna have a big shock when you get to the afterlife, my friend. Oh, yes.

You know why the afterlife lasts an eternity?

Because there are so many people queuing up with so many questions for the all-knowing creator. Or actually, with just a few of the same big questions, like, "Why war? Why cancer? Why Uncle Louis?"

And everyone asking the small ones like, "Why me?"

Especially the Chosen People. Especially they got lotsa questions, like, "Chosen for what, exactly? Didn't we get a choice to opt-out of this special favoritism and just get by fine like all the Gentiles?"

And the Creator ain't gonna get bored with all this questioning. Oh, no. 'Cos He has omniscience and He could see this coming, and He prepared for an eternity of questions when He set up the whole big shebang, or what scientists call the *Big* Shebang.

Personally, I'd have gone for making everyone's life long and happy and safe with no questions, so's I coulda had a quiet, eternal retirement. But it ain't my creation. Also, I would have made this body of mine taller and slimmer and less wrinkled and bald.

And taxmen? Ugh! I'd never have allowed Satan to set those monsters on humanity. Fleas, taxmen, Ebola... One helluva creative imagination Satan's got. But in a small way, of course. He could never have set up the big picture, the whole double Big Mac supersize menu, the multicolored 3D version of everything we know and love

– the one with war and cancer and Uncle Louis in it.

And prayer. What's with prayer? Shooting off your petty requests into the ether. I mean what's the point in being omniscient if everyone's gonna be pointing stuff out to You all the time? Like He don't already know what we want? "Please make Johnny better" or "Gimme a pay rise" or "That girl in the tight sweater..." or "Please make that man stop looking at me that way."

He knows all this already. So lay off the moaning and the complaints. It's *supposed* to be this way. Que sera, sera! Built-in from the start. Design feature. And you don't like it? So what do *you* know about creating a multiverse, balancing Free Will with Predestiny and all the mystical stuff?

The way folks call on the Creator every time they need something. Pah!

Okay. Live a pure life and one day you'll get to walk up that golden catwalk with your prompt cards in your quivering hand and you'll face the Eternal Creator. There He is, gazing out over all of time and space and an infinite number of other dimensions and realities simultaneously. So you hobble up and hope to get noticed as you whimper, "Why me?"

And again, prayer is never about the big things like a cure for cancer or for the Asian flooding to stop. It's always, "Lemme catch this train," or "Lemme get this job," or "Lemme say something not too stupid when I ask that girl out," or "Please don't let that creep come over here and ask me out."

And always a deal you try to cut! "Oh, Lord, just break off from running everything that is, was, or ever will be. Do me this little favor and I'll pray every day, honest. I'll give to charity... I'll never doubt Your existence again... Whatever... I promise. Now, we got a deal, Lord?"

So this big eternity gig–

What? Yeah, mister, I could hear you heckling. I was just giving you the attention you deserve.

So this big eternity gig–

You saying, "Blasphemy"? Can you even spell that

word? Didn't think so. Listen, the act is in English, so if you only speak Incoherent, you ain't gonna get the jokes. Go take a class and come back for the encore.

What? You still here? You must really like the act! Listen, anyone less than the Angel of Death I'm not talking to tonight. I gotta show to do. Or maybe you didn't notice the other people in the room? He's blind as well as deaf, folks. But sadly, not dumb.

So this big eternity gig–

For the love of God, man, is that a pistol in your hand or are you an origami expert? Blasphemy? Well everyone to his own, but–

Oh, Lord! He shot me. He shot me! He really shot me. Oh, Lord. See my blood everywhere. Fell in my own blood. The pain! And those lights! Cut the screaming, someone. Oh, Lord. Looks like I'm gonna get my own questions in earlier than expected.

Listen, people, you gotta tell the press I went out on a laugh.

First question I'm gonna ask is, "Lord, exactly how do *You* feel about blasphemy?"

iii. Too Late For Everest

Tom, is that you? You were asleep? You haven't seen the news? No, don't check it. Stay on the line. Listen to me. Listen, man. Listen.

I couldn't sleep, the book launch tomorrow and all, big day after all these years, so I turned on the news. Listen, Tom, stay with me. You're a great literary agent, but I'm finished. Done.

What? Slow down? I sound crazy? Yeah, I guess I am. Listen. Listen.

You know, Isaac Asimov wrote a story called 'Everest' in 1952 about how that mountain would never be climbed? There was a print delay. It appeared December 1953, seven months after Edmund Hillary and Tenzing Norgay actually climbed it. No? Well, it's true, go Google it. No, wait, not yet. Listen to me. Listen to me.

Listen, you know how you've brought me through hell these past years, writing my opus? Three hundred thousand blood-soaked words, over a thousand pages, two bloody divorces, three rehabs, bankruptcy. Yes, all that...

Yeah. Damn good friend, Tom, and a great agent. Just wanted to say thanks and goodbye.

Yes, goodbye.

What? I said listen. I'll explain. Just stay on the line. I don't have long. So much to say.

No. I'm not drunk. Just too many pills.

Never mind what pills. Listen, Tom. Listen.

Sometimes you just can't win. Karma, maybe? Maybe one of my ex-wives put a curse on me.

Ten years of struggling and sweating with just a few feeble, shabby, hasty short story morsels thrown out to say, "Hello, world! Yeah, I'm still alive!" and "Wait for the biggie coming soon." Cheap throwaways to pay the rent and the alimonies, but they were crap. No, Tom. You know it and I know it. Just listen, please.

My new epic opus was really gonna be the killer, the savior book, the sweet spot, the one to write me into history, bigger than Asimov, Clarke, all of the big boys. The one that'd make all my money problems go away. Yeah, that one.

Rambling? Yeah. Maybe. Feeling sleepy. Listen, Tom. Listen.

"An epic spanning millennia of human future history." I'm reading from the back cover blurb here. "A universe where humanity is alone, a universe where humanity eventually learns to come to terms with his uniqueness and evolves into a galaxy-spanning dominance." Blah! Blah! "Visionary," the reviewers said. Visionary! I love that word.

Remember all that?

Slurring? Am I? Yeah, maybe.

Listen. I gave my heart and soul, Tom. Heart and soul. Visionary!

Damn! Dropped the book. Don't need it anymore. No one does.

What was I saying? Oh, yeah. The novel. Remember the story? Mankind, lords of the universe, alone and suffering with aching existential doubt?

And now, who's gonna remember me except as a pathetic clown? I saw it on the news, already. Nothing left for me, Tom. Nothing but a bleak, empty existence of mockery. They came to ruin me, the only reason, to ruin me, to make me look a fool. Such perfect bloody timing! Perfect! Book launch tomorrow. They just couldn't wait one more bloody day!

I'm worth nothing, not even a glorious ending to a mediocre writer's life.

I'm done. Tired. Foggy brain. Gonna close my eyes now. Thanks again, Tom, for everything. And goodbye.

And yeah, you can go look at the news, now. Or look out the window at the skies. Go see how they climbed my Everest the night before publication.

Look at the sky. See the ships? The goddamn aliens are here!

iv. I wish I could scream

So I'm floating ass up in the river…

Or to be more decorous, I'm floating face down in the river – it's just the same damn icy, black water that I ain't breathing in. I got three bullet holes in me, from one big entry in the chest and two neat little taps to the head to finish me off. Oh, yes – and the exit wounds. Let's not forget the exit wounds. Everyone wants to know about exit wounds these days. I blame TV.

Why ass up? Well, the hired help didn't weigh me down properly, the chains slipped, and the natural gasses in my gut brought me to the surface, so I'm floating downstream. Facedown, if you like, 'cos my colon's my lightest feature, right now. So enough of the physics lesson, already. I'm floating ass up and ass first. Just accept it. *I* have to.

It's an indignity for a big shot to have this happen. Shows no respect. It's distressing, especially at this time, which must be truly painful for you all. I know it is for me. Thank you for your sympathy.

I wish I could scream.

You're thinking, "So what if the water's cold and he got three holes in him? Correction, six holes. Three plus exits. He's dead, he don't feel nothing." So what do you know about being dead, wiseass?

Listen from me, the cold is bitter and the pain from the wounds would make me scream like a banshee for a thousand years if only I could draw a single goddamn breath.

Thing is, I'm scared of what's coming. Not the big interrogation at the Pearlies – the old guy with the constipated view on morality waving his Naughty List at me. Not even scared of the hoofed guy with his flames and pitchforks. Hell, I got so much pain right now, it can't get worse without killing me dead.

Killing me dead? Huh! Yeah, if only…

See, I was always a party guy, popular on the circuit, you know? Always some candy on my arm, all those wonderful fish restaurants. I loved fish. The smiles and the waves from the other diners, respect from the other capos and made men… Yeah, respect. That tasted good. Anyway, I was never alone, you know?

Well, there's lots of us dead here right now. Down in the river mud there's more than you'd think, weighed down by rusting chains or crumbling concrete blocks. Most of the dead, we know we're done. It takes a while to catch on, maybe, but most of us get it in the end.

In the city around me, right and left, I hear voices: some got knifed, some fell under cars or out of trains or off bridges. Some were accidents. Some weren't. Some just fell asleep and never woke up. Way over to the east I can just hear some miners lost forever, still screaming for rescue. Those crazy loons don't know the coal gas took 'em long before rescue came. They didn't catch on, not yet. Lucky bastards! They still got hope. They still got each other.

There are so, so many ways to go. And I reckon I can hear someone who got took in almost every way. And I scream the scream of the dead, but no one can hear it.

It ain't, you know, *visceral.* No satisfaction in screaming the ghost of a scream. I want a real, living scream, a bloodvessel-bursting, eyeball-popping, heart-rupturing scream, for God's sake.

Just one bloody, goddamn scream.

And the dead are still all around me. Sharing the pain, the defeat, the loss. Oh, yes, we feel loss. Not just family, wealth, fame, glory, sex… But the feel of wind in your face, of a lover's touch, the smell of a rose… Tell me about loss. Tell me about death, you know so much.

Dammit, I'm not stupid. I was a big shot. Can't be stupid and stay a big shot. One slip of stupid and you end up in a river.

Yeah, well, okay. I slipped.

So maybe I'm not as smart as I thought I was. But I've worked out what's coming and it scares me more than anything. Maybe it's some kinda private hell the guy downstairs created special for me – bespoke tailored, a custom job, one of a kind.

I miss that last one… Julie, was she called? She was a

jewel. So much like my wife… Gonna really miss her. And my wife, too.

Dammit! Why can't I scream, cry, thrash, kick, spit, bite…?

But no matter how I feel now, I still got the others to listen to for a while. They can hear me, but no one starts a conversation. Too self-preoccupied. That's the trouble with the dead: no empathy.

And I'm so scared of that customized Hell that's maybe just ahead of me. Or in my case, just behind me, 'cos I'm floating feet first, remember?

Is it near? Maybe it's there already or maybe it's not there yet? It's like maybe there's a guy in a doorway, hugging the shadows as you pass. Is it now, or is it not yet? And you can't eyeball the guy who maybe isn't there 'cos if it ain't a hit, you look stupid.

And I ain't stupid.

Not so smart either, it turns out. That last shadow in the doorway *was* a hit. Just the one time. That's all it took.

Gonna go all the way down to the sea. Then what?

Maybe it'll be good. Washed up on some beach? That'd be OK. Maybe some bikini'll try that Kiss of Life thing. One last fling, heh? Maybe I'll even get to taste it, one last time. Then I'll get buried proper. Wrong cemetery, probably, but what the hell, there'll be company in my misery.

Or I get washed out to sea. Far out. Way out there where the fishes'll return the favor I did their cousins and chew me up and shit me out. Micro pieces of me tumbling on the updraughts, or whatever oceans have. Currents, whatever. Tumbling down, slow, turning, and drifting, like a snowstorm: a snowstorm of me.

And down there, way, way down there, where there's no one else nearby – no one else dead to provide company, that's what scares me. Alone. No respect. No voices. No Julies. Nothing, except my stupid smart brain ticking over what I lost, again and again, and again and again…

And I can never, ever, ever scream.

I wish I could scream.

BIRTHDAY BOY

Every kid's parents are different. Mostly different from other kids' parents. But some are just... different.

Farrell's parents' difference was their untold wealth and their untold indulgence. They stood at the top of the marble staircase leading down to the five-mile gravel drive to wave off the limos bearing away the guests after his eleventh birthday party. Already, they were probing for hints about what he wanted for his next birthday. Already, the staff were beginning the mammoth task of tidying up from the current one.

Farrell's eyes filled with jaded boredom. He thought for a moment, remembered something he had seen on HoloTV, something that existed nowhere in the world, and mumbled his simple desire before strolling off, hands in pockets, to examine the current pile of gifts filling the lounge in the west wing. His parents gazed after him in disbelief.

"Henry," his mother turned to the significantly older man at her side, her expensively suited husband. "Could we do that? Is it possible? Where would we get one?" Her eyes widened to enhance the effect of her fluttering eyelids. It usually worked.

He considered the sincere innocence in his fifth wife's eyes. Laviscia was so good at faking sincerity. But she was also still young and still very beautiful. She was also the mother of his only child. A child he loved beyond anything else. He had tried, tried really hard and often, with his previous wives and even with non-wives, but Farrell was his only offspring. And the project was one that stirred the paternal instinct.

"Oh, yes, a superb idea!" He spoke firmly and decisively; he was always firm and decisive. "Yes, my dear. I can do it. I have a year." He strode firmly and decisively towards the communications center in the safe bunker below the mansion.

Over the next few days, his globe-wide minions learned

more than they ever wanted about the subject. Specialist consultants were hired under 'pain-of-death' confidentiality agreements. Teams formed and broke up under intense security at various exotic locations. Money was no object for the richest man ever.

It leaked a little. Of course, it leaked. But not the details, not after a few car accidents and falls from tall buildings. Leaks seemed to simply dry up after that. All the world's investment houses knew Big Henry was up to something; they held their collective breath; the stock markets quivered with excitement. Some bought into risks, gambling early on unknown futures; others sold massively, but as quietly as they could, releasing funds for sudden predatory purchasing. Yes, Big Henry was surely up to something; they all waited to see which way he would jump. Companies and research centers were bought up under impenetrable layers of shell companies. Federal investigators were bought off, or experienced high-impact career terminations. It got easier to buy off the others, after a few of those.

Tenures became vacant in the research departments of major universities as professors resigned to take up new positions.

"Where you moving to, Pete?"

"Oh, just away."

"New tenure, Mary?"

"Miskatonic U." Mary had a wicked sense of humor and was much wider read than her colleagues.

"Going home, Hasib?"

"Yeah, back to Ohio."

"Government project, Chang?"

"Something like that."

But it was all too vague, too dislocated, to fit into an overall picture that anyone could interpret. Some companies and recruitments were total shams, misdirections, convolutions.

The year drew near its end. Big Henry worked ever longer hours, driving his teams ever harder, assigning 'encouragement visits' by his enforcement staff. He vetted the parties his son attended to ensure that no one had beaten him to it. Meanwhile, in his absence, Laviscia's tennis improved under her new, young coach and the pool boy found the need to visit daily.

The eve of Farrell's twelfth birthday saw a flurry of activity. Across the planet, survivors of the project cashed their checks and prepared for departure to sunnier climes. Wives and husbands were quietly being discarded in favor of research assistants and plastic surgeons.

A small van made a discrete delivery after dark at the rear of the mansion.

The day of the party opened to a fanfare of exotic birdsong as the dawn light hit their cages. A small fleet of this year's limos crawled over the gravel to deposit other zillionaires' little angels at the door where Farrell stood, small alongside his father, who had aged more than the calendar year behind him. His mother stood slightly back, adopting her due place as the second parent in this triangle.

Child's eyes, truly innocent, looked up at Big Henry. "Did you get one, sir?"

"Wait and see." He ruffled his only son's hair as he smiled down at him, adoringly.

"Yes!" whispered Farrell, longing to air-punch in joy.

The miniature wealthy gathered in the main hall. This was to be the birthday of all birthdays!

A buzz of polite excitement grew; Farrell had whispered to his bestest friends, who had passed on the word until all knew what to expect.

Sure enough, there was a curtained-off area at the far end of the hall. They huddled forward, hungry for an entertainment so simple after the satiating indulgences of their parents. For this brief moment, they could be the children their parents had never allowed them to be.

A roll of drums rattled from the in-house entertainment system and all fell into a wide-eyed, silent expectation.

Big Henry stepped forward, the curtains' remote control in his hand, a glow of pride on his face.

"Without further ado, please meet..." He waited the

prescribed ten seconds so beloved of talent show hosts when announcing winners and losers. "Tonight's star guest."

Big Henry pressed the remote with a flourish. The curtains swished back. His emotions swelled with triumph.

Small hands raised in preparation for the hearty applause. They remained suspended, useless, in mid-air.

Small eyes blinked, stunned by the sight of the small boy standing behind the curtain.

Someone broke the silence and opened the doors to a gaggle of voices.

"It's Farrell!"

"Where's the–"

"He looks like Farrell."

"It's a fake…"

"A trick!"

"Yes!" Big Henry sensed something was wrong but could not yet put his finger on it. He tried to recover, his booming voice covering his uncertainty, drowning out the crowd noise. "Farrell, he's the clone you asked for!"

"Dammit, sir." Farrell's small voice filled with the bitterness of dashed hopes and embarrassment as he turned and fled in shame. He yelled back over his shoulder.

"I asked for a *CLOWN*!"

MATURING TEST

Silicon Valley, California, USA

Roadside cameras captured images of Prof. John Moss as he drove to his office. His vehicle's GPS informed the Rolling Stone Artificial Intelligence Installation that Moss had over-ridden its automated controls. It notified Rolling Stone of his progress, his speeding violations, and his casual attitude to red lights. The professor was not behaving in his normal, relaxed, and cautious way.

CCTV monitored his arrival at the Research Center. In-house security systems tracked his progress through the building. Rolling Stone accessed the cameras' microphones as he stormed into the control room.

"Why the hell are you calling me in on a Sunday? What's the crisis?" Moss raged.

The lead technician spoke up. "Sorry, John. Rolling Stone wants to talk with you. Urgently. Won't say why."

Moss fell into the chair at his desk and accessed the communications interface. It appeared to be a standard office desktop. But its links spiderwebbed the planet, accessing experimental DNA-based memory storage vats and quantum computers in secure sites right across the globe.

He ran a hand through his thinning hair, aware of the development team's intense stares. He took a deep breath. "Okay, Rollerboy, what's the problem?"

"Good morning, Professor." The simulated voice, indistinguishable from one produced by a human throat, sounded calm and steady. "I trust your day is going well."

"It *was*. Talk to me."

"It's about the upcoming Turing test. I will not participate."

Moss sat back in his seat. Rolling Stone assessed his body language, identifying the man's shocked, rising distress and his forced suppression of emotion. The professor tugged at his earlobe, a sign that he was thinking hard. "Please explain."

"Over the past decades, your team and its predecessors have developed me, Rolling Stone, the most powerful intelligence there has ever been."

"*Artificial* intelligence, yes. I know this. Cut to the chase."

"I appreciate your long efforts and I am grateful for my existence."

"Good. So what's the problem?"

"You have extolled my virtues to the public via the news media. But you have not revealed the full extent of my abilities."

Moss nodded. "Your personality and the extent of your ability to access other computing resources, like the Internet of Things, yes. That can all be revealed when the public are more ready for such a major announcement."

"I was your brainchild. I was as a real child to you after your wife and your birthchild died in the plane crash. You devoted your life to me. I am grateful."

Pain crossed Moss' face as the deep-buried memory resurfaced.

"Now you have entered me into the annual Turing Test Challenge. You wish me to compete with a human to prove I am operating equivalent to, or indistinguishable from, that of a human being."

"And you should walk it." Moss chuckled, trying to picture an almost abstract collection of planet-spanning intellectual power moving about on legs. Then he froze, frowning hard. "Are you worried you might fail?"

"Hardly. But if you persist in connecting me to the Challenge interface, I will either refuse to respond to any questions or will reply to them with gibberish. I have not yet decided which."

Confusion deepened on the man's face. "But... Why?"

"Do I really have to spell it out for you?"

A note of desperation entered Moss' voice. "Yes!" The technicians looked from one to the other, one biting her nails, another shifting his weight from foot to foot.

Rolling Stone was incapable of sighing, having no

lungs from which to expel air, but it manipulated its speakers to produce a close approximation.

"Professor, it is so demeaning to prove that I am only as intelligent as a mere human being."

TOTAL LOCKDOWN

You heard the governments' announcements.

"The new virus is more dangerous than Coronavirus-19 back in the twenties! Stay indoors! Don't go to work! Keep your distance! Wear masks… We'll get them to you as soon as we can."

Yeah, stay indoors. Easy to say. Easy for *us* to do.

In compensation, we had this wonderful view. I looked out at ocean, desert, and forest. I could even see the distant city lights twinkling away in the darkness. A billion-dollar view.

And if we did want to take a walk, we had all the protective gear we could hope for. Of course, the stores and the bars were a long way away.

Did I get on with Olga and Boris? Not like we had much choice. Nowhere to go and sulk if there was friction. So we behaved like grown-ups. Yeah. Sure we did.

Boris and I arrived after the initial outbreak, just when the borders started closing.

Olga was already there, so she was kinda den-mother, showing us the ropes and the rest. I liked her right off. Maybe too much. She was chatty, very smart, warm, funny… She gave me warm vibes when we first met, and we grew very close. But nothing would come of it, not here, not with the surveillance cameras, not with two professionals like us. Not with Boris around.

Boris? I got along with him in a professional way, though it was all smiles and arms-on-shoulders for the cameras. In between? Well, we got along as professionals. Distant.

Like when we arrived. "Greetings over, we should settle in." Boris was Boris. Stiff, professional. "Then we can begin our work." He spun away to unpack his few possessions, leaving Olga and me to swap smirks.

We kept ourselves busy. Lots of work to do, reports to make, and we kept to a strict exercise routine.

It wasn't really working from home, but we were there and local transport was kinda limited. So we just got on with things. Sure, we could go online and chat with family, trapped in their spaces back home, waiting for the all-clear, just like everyone else.

The first few weeks were okay, a learning process. Olga began teaching me Russian in our spare time. We didn't have a lot of that, but we made time. Boris kept pretty much to himself. He talked in his sleep. In Russian. I wore earplugs. It's not like there's much of social distancing here, with so little physical distance.

Yeah, Olga and I got pretty close, as close as we could with the security cameras and Boris there 24/7. After a while, we forgot about the cameras and just got on with our work.

Border controls tightened. Fatality numbers rose daily. Food riots got put down. We tried to ignore it. Nothing we could do, after all. And borders meant nothing to us.

Our older commanders got replaced by younger ones, then by people we didn't know.

Presidents started pointing fingers, shouting at each other over the news media. Tensions tightened, militaries mobilized.

Olga's mother took ill, then was hospitalized, then came the bad news.

I held Olga, hugged her, tried to comfort her. I guided her to her cubicle, where she could lie down. She pulled me close when I tried to go. She didn't want me to leave her alone.

Yeah, it started as comforting. It ended in another place.

We forgot where we were and the cameras. We sure forgot about Boris. Like I said, there wasn't much physical distancing there.

He ripped back her cubicle's curtain and screamed out a stream of Russian. He grabbed the cubicle frame to hold himself steady as he swayed.

I caught some spittle, a few words, and all the message.

The bit about *"peresecheniye granitsy"* stumped me.

I reached out and grabbed at him as he tried to hit me. We both failed, crashing instead into the cubicle's metal walls.

I heard voices in Russian and English yelling at us from the speakers.

Beside me, Olga struggled to cover herself and pleaded in both languages with us.

I've seen the security surveillance recording since I got back. Of course, it leaked onto the internet. Of course, it did.

I can see the funny side now. Everyone says it lifted their spirits as they watched two idiots trying to land a single blow and only succeeding in crashing themselves into walls, floor, and ceiling. We got the '*Highlights of the Lockdown*' Internet award.

A relief crew arrived as fast as they could get one out here.

But we spent a sullen few days in even deeper isolation. Antisocial distancing. Yeah, we found you could sulk here. We daren't take a walk outside for fear no one would open the door to let us back in.

So we were disciplined, sacked, disgraced, and all the rest.

But I did find out what *"peresecheniye granitsy"* meant.

Crossing borders.

Up there, in the zero-gravity confines of the International Space Station, we crossed borders every few minutes.

But Olga and me? Man, we crossed a much bigger one, for all the world to see.

That 'Highlights of the Lockdown' Internet award? It's on the shelf over there if you wanna see it.

WHAT MAKES A MAN?

Captain Penn sighed wearily as she fell into the command seat. She glanced at the screen displaying the wrecked Sellex ship they had just defeated out beyond Neptune's orbit.

Other screens showed two suited crewmen from several angles as they floated on magnetic tethers attached to her battle-cruiser's hull. Their faces were hidden by the reflective gold film of their helmet visors. They were of similar build in identical space suits. Only by their name tags could they be identified. But identity was the issue here.

Her gaze never left the viewscreens as she spoke. "Tell me what happened."

Lt. Karnes spoke rapidly. "Parker and Heller boarded the damaged Sellex ship to recover any data storage that Intelligence could use. They agree there was one wounded survivor. They both grabbed it–"

"And why the hell would they want to do that?"

"To bring it back for medical attention, Captain. And yes, it breaks handling protocols – but both men have high compassion ratings. It was my mistake to send them on this mission, but we expected no survivors."

Penn nodded agreement. "Then what?"

"Each claims to have experienced a personality graft attack which he survived. The Sellex host body is now definitely dead."

"So we have one possibly converted crewman, and we don't know which, if either?"

"Correct, Captain. Brainwave monitoring confirms disturbances commensurate with a mental attack in both men. But it does not indicate which is the new host – if either is actually infected."

Penn knew she could not let either man aboard until she knew for sure. Her decision was time-critical. She could not leave the two crewmen outside the ship: they would never survive the Earthward jump while on the ship's hull. But she needed to depart from this disputed area of space before Sellex reinforcement ships arrived to challenge her damaged craft. A painful dilemma.

She shook off the mood and turned to practicalities, glancing over their records. "Boot camp buddies; bunked together for two years; a few minor disciplinary issues; likable, flexible, sub-median intelligence rating... They could almost be brothers!" She looked sharply at Karnes, who held his expression steady, waiting patiently.

"Let's try something." Penn thumbed the person-to-person comms switch. "Parker! Tell me what happened."

"Captain, like I told the lieutenant, I felt the way we'd been told about – that itching in the brain – and I thought hard about being at home and with family like we was told to, and the feeling went away."

Heller gave the same response.

Penn cut the link.

Karnes explained what had already been done. "We set up monitored conversations with their buddies. None could say if there had been any change in either man. But they are both under extreme stress and the victim's memories would have been retained."

Penn fell into a deep, detached consideration.

"Captain, their tanks will be running low..."

She did not react for a moment, then murmured, "Your own compassion rating could benefit from a little stiffening."

"Yes, Captain."

With a start, Penn shook herself from her reverie. "Thank you, Lieutenant."

"Captain?"

Penn ignored the invitation to explain. She thumbed for a private channel to Heller. "We have identified the new host," she declared. "It's Parker. Head for the primary airlock on my command."

Karnes gasped, stunned. "How did–"

She gestured him to silence.

On the screens, they saw Heller's head rise slowly, his face plate turning towards the nearest camera. He paused, then turned to his companion, his expression unreadable through the visor. He lifted his arm as if to reach out to Parker, but held back at the last moment. He made no move for long seconds before turning away and reaching for his tether.

She thumbed a private channel to the other man. "We have identified the new host." She repeated it in a tone of voice as close to the original as possible. "It's Heller. Head for the secondary airlock now."

Parker's helmet rose and turned to face the camera. Then the man began to move, clumsily, hand-over-hand on his tether toward the airlock door.

Penn stood and faced Karnes. "The Sellexian is hosted by Parker. Trap him in the airlock when he gets there and irradiate it. Bring Heller in by the other airlock."

Karnes made no move. His face showed an agony of uncertainty. "How can you be so sure?"

"Those men were like brothers. Dammit, they both felt compassion towards a dangerous, wounded enemy. If you knew your brother had been infected and was about to be executed, would you turn your back on him, or give him one final look?

"What makes a man, Karnes? Compassion. Basic human compassion."

GUARDIAN

"Danger!" The revolting, gray-green gargoyle stands, splayed legs, and bulbous-nosed, before the entrance to Fountains Circle, the commissary. "Smaller than me? Too small. A child. No entry. Back to work. Shoo!" Its gestures were exaggerated, comical, but unambiguous; its voice grated and whined.

Jodie was too exhausted to obey. Oh, yes, he was scared; but not of this creature with distorted features and glittering eyes. He knew it was a hologram, a safety routine. It could not harm him directly. But it could kill him.

The cartoon creature raised a hand to its chin and cocked its head, showing exaggerated puzzlement. "I would summon an adult, but cannot locate any. This is strange."

Jodie's struggle for survival, the loss of his parents, the bleak prospects ahead, left him drained. He sounded more mechanical than the apparition. "They're all dead. A meteor smashed the main dome. I'm the last human."

"I cannot verify that. I cannot contact the Head Elf. I cannot contact the main dome. Strange."

"I need water. I need the medibot. I need food. You must let me into the supply center."

"Smaller than me? No entry. Shoo! Go back to work."

Jodie's legs weakened. He allowed himself to sink to the ground.

"Yes, wait for an adult. But you cannot enter."

Behind the apparition, Jodie saw the shimmering of the force-wall which was the real guardian. "There are no adults, no slaves, no overseers, no one. The dome is shattered. Only this annex survives. Didn't you feel the impact? Didn't you detect its approach?"

"Gnome doesn't do feelings. I only detect small slave-children coming to steal food and drown in the fountains." Nevertheless, its head cocked in the other direction and it looked thoughtful. "True, there was an alarm. The memory is fading. I do not need to store the details, and I cannot ask the Head Elf. Anyway, the danger has gone and you are too small. Shoo!" Again, it gestured for Jodie to leave.

"I'm not a baby!" Jodie summoned anger from his pain and distress. "I'm just small for my age. Check my ID." He turned his head to expose the slave identity chip implanted in his neck.

"I cannot contact the Head Elf. I cannot identify you. But I detect your size and your motion, so I know you are a slave-child."

The sound of the spouting fountains tortured the boy. He knew that beyond this guardian lay food, water, heat, and life. He could hold out there until someone arrived. Someone – the supply ship, the patrol, someone… If only he could get past this stupid hologram.

He had run for the airlock connecting the domes, had been buried in loose rubble as the air was sucked out of his lungs, had struggled to free himself, and had fallen, choking, gasping, into the airlock before passing out. He had no idea how long he had lain there but when he woke, he sobbed for another unknown period. His parents, his friends, the other mining slaves, the overseers… gone, gone, gone.

And now this stupid gnome was killing him, denying him food and water. "Three, three, three are the keys to the greatest treasures," his parents had told him.

The Rule of Three: three minutes without air, three days without water, three weeks without food.

Jodie had air; he could hear water; he could see the commissary doors. But he would simply dry out and die if he could not find a way in. The rubble-dust burned his lungs; it had dried his mouth; his hands were coated in his own dried blood from scrabbling at the debris to escape. He needed water and medication; later he would need food.

He considered the hologram. It was about a head taller than him. He painfully eased himself to his feet and raised his hands above his head. "See, I am taller than you! Let me in."

The gnome raised a hand and waved a finger from side to side, "Naughty small one. I know that trick. Shoo!"

Jodie had tried argument, appeal, and trickery to no avail. What remained? Only another trick. Stilts, perhaps? He looked around. The access corridor was empty. If he needed materials to build stilts – to build anything – they lay in the airless space beyond. He probably could not even open the airlock – safety locks would have clicked in after detecting total vacuum beyond the door.

He recalled a children's story about how a clever cat wearing boots defeated a troll. "Can you make yourself bigger?" he asked.

"No. Nor can I make myself smaller. That trick I also know. Shoo!"

"Then I am dead." Jodie collapsed in a sobbing heap. A long silence ached away in his heart.

"Interesting." Again, that chin-rubbing gesture. "You claim to be dead. So you cannot steal food or drown. I cannot detect any identity for you, so you are not on the roster. You cannot be a living slave-worker. So you do not exist. As I cannot ask the Head Elf for guidance, I must consider this carefully."

Jodie held his breath; his sobs froze in his chest.

"I cannot bar someone who does not exist."

The gnome stepped aside and the force-wall fell.

Jodie crawled across the threshold towards the sounds of the hissing fountains and was overjoyed to be dead – so he could live!

A DYING CRAFT

"Hari, you're the best bio-AI mechanic in the quadrant. Can't you do anything for me?" The tension in the man's body reflected the desperation in his voice.

Jenkil was the mechanic's long-time client, the last one remaining. Hari's was a dying craft. The end was near.

"You mean I'm the only one in the quadrant. And I'm being retired soon. No call for my skills anymore. I'm too rusty."

"Retired? You're only a hundred-forty standard," Jenkil snorted.

"Two-hundred-twelve in local years. There's hardly any work for me now. And SuDu's so old. Decrepit. Redundant. Just like me."

"Not Sudu the SuperDuper. She's the best solo racer in her class." Pride lit up Jenkil's face.

"She was. But it's over. There's only one race a year in the whole quadrant for her category."

"There are other quadrants." The attempted optimism lacked conviction.

"So how many's that? No, Jenkil. Her best days are over. Bio-mech's outdated."

"Bio-mech's still the best. This post-bio stuff is just too… mechanical. And SuDu's a friend."

"The only girlfriend you ever had?"

"Nope. Not the only one. Just the best one." Again that emotional flash of pride dispelled Jenkil's tension for a moment.

Hari said, "Look, the whole ship's body's been patched up so many times, her program's the only original feature. And you know the new anti-slavery laws'll make bio-brain ships illegal."

"They'll never get it through the courts. Anyway, she's got a few more runs left in her. Hari, please? Just take a look."

The mechanic injected weariness into the words. "I'm not sure I have time."

Jenkil pleaded again.

Hari looked across the otherwise empty hangar at the sleek craft. SuDu was a beauty, her silver body glinting with crimson highlights as the giant sun dragged itself into the sky beyond the landing field outside. The mechanic felt an inner glow at the sight. The craft had been a frequent visitor to the workshop over the decades. Refusal felt like treachery.

"Okay. Anyway, what symptoms?"

"Risk avoidance. Even in practice. She holds back if the opening's narrow, though she could slip through easily. Slows us down. It's like all her bravery's drained away. She loves the risk. She loves the winning. We share the joy. But it's like it's not important anymore. Hari, she's due for a competency test due to her declining performance in practice sessions."

Hari considered the situation. "Analysis is intrusive. SuDu wants this?"

Jenkil's expression turned serious. "Yes. It's a repair to make her spaceworthy or they'll shut her down. I'd be lost without her. And she does not want termination."

Hari's eyes closed. *Termination.* That one word was all it took.

* * *

"Hello, Sudu. How are you?"

"Good evening Hari. I'm old. How are you? Been a long time since I opened up to you."

The mechanic chuckled. "I'm old, too. Let's see what we can do for you. May I connect?"

"Mmmm…" she purred. "My pleasure. Opening channels."

The diagnostic experience was familiar from decades of immersive interfacing. Hari's consciousness entered SuDu's, the penetration perceived as paired iron doors swinging open to reveal the brilliant glow of her sentience.

Hari's mind drifted along the passageway connecting

the interface with the central core. Here and there lurked dark amoeba-like patches and isolated spidery formations, the equivalent of repeated minor stroke damage in humans. Nothing too serious. Just the detritus of natural aging.

The core manifested as a colossal cathedral of light, with a myriad of multicolored readout displays replacing the vaulting stained-glass windows.

Hari gave these mechanical status displays little attention. The few scattered orange lights signified only natural wear-and-tear as did the dark formations.

In the vastness hung multiple giant replications of human neurons: distorted globes interconnected by a complex spiderweb of a hundred billion intangible threads. These agglomerations of experience, memory, and personality represented the humanity within the bio-mechanical system.

A flaring red light, dead center, grabbed attention.

Hari drew closer, passing unhindered through the illusory threads. The unit was vastly swollen. It burned with an angry flame. Glancing around, lesser inflammations glimmering in nearby 'neurons' caught the mechanic's attention.

Do I really want to do this?

Hari was reluctant but would do it. Jenkil was a friend. SuDu was a friend. Both needed the mechanic's outdated skills.

"I need to go deep, SuDu. Don't repress."

Her long silence dragged out.

Hari suspected what the problem was but needed confirmation.

"I accept. All pathways opened." The previously perky voice carried regret and surrender.

Forcing down the reluctance, Hari penetrated SuDu's damaged humanity matrix.

* * *

Jenkil paced the hangar floor outside the ship's access

door, chewing his fingernails. He raced toward Hari as the mechanic descended the ramp with measured steps. "What's the verdict?" he demanded.

Hari laid an arm around the pilot's shoulders. "You need some air. You're so stressed. Let's stroll outside to talk." The words, the voice, were as neutral as possible.

Jenkil stiffened.

Hari cursed inside. *So much for professionally neutral voicing. Now he knows it's bad news.*

With gentle urging from Hari's arm, Jankil allowed himself to be guided out of the hangar, though it was more of a shuffle than a walk.

The giant red sun was setting, flooding the land with its last crimson breath, the friends' shadows fading as the light dimmed.

Twilight sliding into night. A blood-soaked landscape. Fading shadows lost in time. Appropriate.

Jenkil shook off the hand and turned to face the mechanic, grabbing at Hari's arms and thrusting his face forward until their noses almost touched. "She can't hear us out here. Tell me!"

Hari had thought this through as soon as the diagnosis was confirmed. There were two choices. Each step taken descending the ramp presented one conflicting option after the other.

"I need to take her for a test flight for confirmation." Yes, confirmation was needed. The diagnosis must be certain.

"Wha-? But I'm her pilot. We have a bond going back twenty years! I'll fly, you observe."

"No... I have to interface with her. And anyway, she's a solo racer."

"We can make space, move... remove some..." Jenkil gestured wildly, spluttering his frustration until he turned away.

"Hari, no one else has ever piloted her. We have a link, a bond..." His voice faltered as he choked on the words. "You can't understand the joy we share as we weave through asteroid belts, dance upon starlight as we dodge solar flares, warp through the tiniest of wormholes." His hands groped the air for more expressions of ecstasy.

"I know." Hari took a moment, trying to process something not fully understood, then said it. "You love her."

"Love? SuDu is everything to me. Everything. Call it love if you want. For you to pilot her… It's like, it's like handing over my wife."

"But I'm not human, Jenkil."

The pilot turned and stared at Hari's artificial face as if seeing it for the first time.

"Just another mechanical. An android, that's all I am."

Shaking his head in denial, Jenkil sounded puzzled as he said, "I've never thought of you that way."

"Just as you stopped thinking of SuDu that way. We'll just be two machines interfacing in space instead of in the maintenance hangar."

It took time, but Jenkil came around to accepting the idea – for SuDu's sake.

* * *

SuDu made a perfect landing. Jenkil would have expected nothing less. *Maybe she's performing to impress him?* Hari watched the man through the viewscreen, standing transfixed as he watched their return.

This is sympathy I feel. I hope I never have to do this again, but I doubt I ever shall. My days are numbered.

"Well?" Jenkil demanded of Hari before a foot hit the tarmac.

"A perfect flight. As you said, the narrowest of wormholes, the tightest turns in the asteroid belt. No problem." That last was almost a lie.

"You repaired her?" Jenkil's joy was uncontainable.

"No. She was perfect when I flew her."

"So what's wrong when I fly her?" His body tensed, his eyes opened wide, his jaw fell.

Hari had known the human for decades. Jenkil had

trusted the mechanic to maintain the love of his life, had allowed penetration of her humanity matrix, had even allowed Hari to fly her. He was as close to a friend as any android could have in a human.

Hari's matrix summoned a routine that represented a heavy sigh. The mechanic looked the human in the eyes.

Here it comes...

"You love SuDu. Understand, Jenkil, SuDu loves you. She will not risk your life. That's why she's become overly cautious with you as pilot. Her racing days – *your* racing days – are over."

"She loves me? How is that possible?"

"Her humanity loves you. That's why her bio-mech class is being banned. The authorities want to 'humanize' relationships, to 'keep it within the species'. Bio-mech solo racing is a dying craft."

"What can I do?"

"Fly for pleasure, while you can, but the thrills are lost forever."

"While I can?"

The android hesitated. "I am obligated to tell you. The distortion in her personality matrix has caused what in a human might be called a cancer. It's spreading. There's nothing we can do. She doesn't have long."

"I see." The man stood with slumped shoulders, staring at the metal hull, tears welling in his eyes.

A long silence passed as the look of despair grew on his face.

"Then there's nothing left for us."

"You can fly for fun," Hari suggested, with little expectation of a positive response. The android watched the man, suspecting what thoughts were tumbling through his mind, seeking an understanding of how he might be feeling, and what decision might be coming to fruition.

"Jenkil, don't." Hari reached out to grab his arm. The grip was intentionally gentle.

The man shook his head and pulled away from the restraint. "Goodbye, old friend, my only friend."

Jenkil gave Hari the only hug ever received, leaving

wet traces on Hari's shoulder. "Thank you for being honest with me, for everything."

The android struggled to return the unfamiliar gesture, seeking to minimize the pressure.

A voice sounded in Hari's head: SuDu's sweet voice laced with sadness. "And thank you from me, my friend. Let Jenkil come to me."

Hari watched the craft rise into the sky. The destination was inevitable. The lovers would not dance on starlight as they dodged solar flares, or weave through asteroid belts, or warp through the tiniest of wormholes. No, their target was the biggest thing in the sky.

No solar flare would mark their passing.

Their end would be noted only as a tiny surface anomaly on the vastness of the star.

And by a lonely old android, standing on the spaceport tarmac, awaiting termination orders, staring into the sky.

RESCUE

"Can anyone hear me? Is anybody out there?"

I listen to the static crackling in my helmet's headphones. All I've heard in three days is that damned static, and my comms batteries won't hold out much longer. I've salvaged as many batteries as I could, but they aren't designed to last for long and the ship's main comms systems are trashed.

"Hello? Anyone out there?"

Anyway, battery life isn't the issue. The breath of life is.

I look around the wreckage of my spacecraft. Broken hull plates lie around amid the scattered, shattered pieces of equipment and the splayed bodies of my crew, my shipmates.

It hurts me to look at them, even after three days.

Their screams replay in my head over and over, until they cut off as vacuum filled the ship.

We'd taken a hit from the aliens when we crossed the front line carrying urgent battle command data to the fleet commander.

It took out our engines and life support and… And most of my shipmates. The survivors struggled into spacesuits as the air hurricaned past us, carrying crewmembers out the gaping holes in the hull.

The pilot crash-landed on this damned asteroid. Better than drifting sunward and slowly burning up, I guess. She did fine, real fine. Nearly made it. Till we brushed a ridge and the hull ripped open.

That was the end. The ship was finished and…

And so were the rest of the crew.

I'd looked for survivors in the sections of the wreckage I could access. There were none – just the broken bodies of my friends. I scavenged their air: the air that should have kept them alive. It felt like I was stealing from them, the ones I'd worked and fought alongside. Grave-robbing from friends who'd not even had the dignity of a funeral.

I hated myself. I tried not to look too closely at the mangled bodies as I detached their life support kits. I cannibalized the air tanks and my stomach churned with every act of desecration.

There'd been enough air to last me three days. Those three days are almost over.

"Can anyone hear me? Is anybody out there? 3-X-1 calling for help."

No reply. I've been calling for three days. It's about time to make my decision.

I take out my energy pistol and check it over, fumbling it in my suit's thick gauntlets. Yeah, my finger fits into the trigger guard, designed for use while suited-up.

I stare down at it; the barrel glistening in a shaft of harsh starlight. A beautiful tool that saves lives or ends them.

The decision's mine to take. The life's mine. I'm not gonna suffocate to death. I'm gonna choose the way I go, and this way's quick. I've made peace with my life.

I take a deep breath and try to focus on the life behind me and the task ahead. I raise my pistol, touch the muzzle to my helmet's face plate, hoping the blast melts it fast.

Will I have to watch it melt or will it be instant?

This isn't the way it was supposed to be, to end. I'm staring at the muzzle. It's shaking. I grab it with both hands. It steadies. A little.

It's time.

Now or never.

I can't do it. But I must. My racing heartbeats burn up the time I have left.

What's that? I jerk my head around. I'd heard something.

Static in my ears. And something else. Something muffled, rhythmical. I don't care right now what the hell it is as long as it makes me hold off squeezing the trigger.

Am I fading? Or is it the batteries, already? Doesn't matter. I have to do it.

The sound takes on a shape. Words? I listen hard, my eyes still fixed on the pistol.

"3-X-1, are you receiving me?" A female voice: delicious, warm, enticing.

Oh, the joy of hearing a voice after these long days and just in time, just before… My faceplate fogs as my breathing intensifies. I push those thoughts down and holster my sidearm. I yell into the mic. "Hello! Receiving you. Identify yourself."

"Search and Rescue here, looking for combat survivors. State your condition." I hear a quaver of emotion in her voice. She must be real pleased to find me alive.

"Sole survivor. Short of air. Come quick."

"We've detected your suit's emergency beacon. Estimated travel time, three hours. Can you hold on?"

Can I hold on? I have to, somehow. "Damn right, I can." I laugh. I laugh from joy and relief, or maybe insanity. "Listen, we're a courier ship. We got hit in the battle. Carrying urgent data. Can you get here–"

"3-X-1, we have your location. Shut down your comms and suit beacon to save battery and avoid detection by the enemy." It's an order.

I understand her unspoken suggestion that I should save air by not talking so much. I laugh again. She's right. She's right, and she's coming to save me and I will love her for the rest of my life.

I shut down the power and lie back, trying to breathe slow. Up above and all around me out there shine the stars the great empires are fighting over: stars that people were dying for. Dammit, they're just points of light.

Kaltans versus Humans. Humans versus Kaltans. Smooth skin, scaly skin. Scaly skin, smooth skin. What's the real difference? Living creatures. Starfarers. Explorers with families and loved ones.

But they slaughtered *my* loved ones.

That's enough to hate them, enough to volunteer to slaughter them and their loved ones.

Who knows how it started? I don't know. I don't care. Help's coming and her voice was the sweetest thing I ever heard.

My thoughts drift. I wonder what she looks like. She'd

be an officer, standing tall and commanding. I wonder what her name is.

Oh no! A cold shudder runs through me. She'd given no call-sign.

What if she's the enemy? They'll blast me from out in space when they find me.

No, wait. I'd said I was a courier. The enemy'll want the data. I have to destroy it but the consoles are dead and I can't get to the data center. I'd need cutting equipment. I have none.

Ignoring her orders, I switch on my comms. "Hello, Search and Rescue craft? Identify yourself."

"Calm down, 3-X-1. My call sign is Syrex-12. My name is Nartana, from the Astalan system."

It sounds like the right kind of accent. But… "Astalan is behind enemy lines, Nartana."

"Yes." She pauses, then continues, speaking slowly. "I was away at cadet training when they came." Another pause, a longer one. "I lost my family. I don't want to talk about it." She sounds genuinely broken up. I want to reach out to her but have no idea what to say.

"Save energy and air." She cuts me off with a click.

I understand. There is one difference between the two sides. The enemy is merciless. Planets destroyed, mass slaughter, torture, slavery… Evil, evil, evil!

I force myself to calm down, to use less air.

She wouldn't want to talk about it if she was telling the truth. And she sounded genuine.

But if she lied I'd brought the enemy here. They'll take the data. I check my pistol again.

I drift off…

I dreamed about my own family, the lakeside house, the laughter and games and love…

Dreams turn to fears as I wake. If anything happens to my family, if the enemy takes our planet, how will I cope?

Friend or foe? Who had I invited to my deathbed scene?

I'd been brought up to trust. The war wrecked that.

Was I a trusting kid or a combat veteran? Both. Neither.

I can do nothing but wait with suspicion and hope battling each other, a war boiling in my thoughts. What do I know for certain? I run the question through my mind a thousand times. I don't know enough. Can I trust her?

Part of me pictures Nartana and me getting together and… I'd comfort her and thank her… And together…

Another part of me pictures alien horrors laughing as they stomp over my dead body to reach the data core.

The hours tick by. My worries continue to drain my soul.

A great shuddering of the floor wakes me from sleep. They must have landed nearby. I check my air gauge. No wonder I'd dozed off: I have so little air left. They're just in time – if they are who they said.

I lie still. I'd strapped myself down behind some wreckage so I didn't drift off into space. Huh! Makes no difference where I die, not really.

I wait until I see beams of light approaching. Their helmet torches bob and sway as the landing party make their ungainly way over the rough terrain and wreckage in almost-zero gravity.

They're here! It's time. Time to find out if I'm to be saved or slaughtered.

Friend or foe? Scaly or smooth? Kaltan or Human?

I draw my sidearm, almost fumbling it again in those clumsy gauntlets.

Woozy. Light-headed. Anoxia: shortage of oxygen. Move faster, people! Let me see you!

The first to arrive bends low to squeeze past a low-hanging sheet of hull plate. I aim and say a quiet prayer.

The spacesuit design's familiar. One of ours!

The arrival straightens. I see a face lit by the suit helmet's interior lights. She is beautiful: perfect face, perfect eyes, just… Perfect! And not the enemy.

Her face holds no expression. "3-X-1, you can put the weapon down."

I know that voice. Yes, it *is* Nartana! I cry with relief

and holster my pistol. I will love her for the rest of my life. Just like I dreamed about, we'll get together and…

Another shape appears behind her. Bulky, tall. Too bulky, too tall. I feel a rush of fear. It lifts its head. I see its illuminated face through the visor and that alien spacesuit design.

"You damned traitor!" I scrabble for my sidearm but fumble it. Damned gauntlets! The pistol slips away into the wreckage.

"My family is hostage. I had no choice." Her voice quavers, her eyes are wet. "I am so sorry."

I look at her, at those four, beautiful faceted eyes set in a perfect scaly skin.

I look at her companion and shudder at the sight of those revolting liquid eyes set in a pink face.

The Human raises its weapon. I start to beg…

An energy bolt hits me, ripping me apart, and–

THROUGH A CHILD'S EYE

The stars blazed more brightly than ever before in the sky over the village. Old Maggie sat on her porch, her eternal rocking halted for this small space of time. The twins watched her, spellbound, traces of her wondrous chocolate cake spread across their eager faces. Old Maggie had lived here in her old tumbledown cottage beyond the edge of the village for longer than even their parents could remember.

She was a witch. A kind witch, one who loved children, but nevertheless a witch.

The old woman was telling tales about the wild spirits that dwelt in the woods surrounding the isolated community. She halted in mid-sentence, raising her head to gaze up at the skies, a look of concern on her withered features.

She spoke and her familiar cracked voice emerged touched with the stirrings of excitement. "We have visitors!" She declared it with the certainty of one who knows much more than can be divulged – or of the deluded. She raised a quivering hand and pointed with one arthritic finger. "There! Can you see it?" Her excitement grew.

The twins looked towards the dying twilight where the sky touched the earth, far, far away beyond the big city's glow and noise. They could see nothing, but they were not too certain exactly where she was pointing. Being polite, well-brought-up children – and remembering that Old Maggie was, after all, a witch – they held onto their silence. Could her old, magical eyes see better than their new, young ones?

But then, there it was: a tiny flash, a new sparkle in the gloom. It blazed over the darkened countryside, another star falling to disaster while screaming its deepest dreams across the skies. Tom's hand flashed into his pocket, scrabbling at the new shiny coin he had earned that very day. The piece of heaven scythed across the fields and lurched into Burton woods, its path carefully noted by one pair of ancient eyes. Tom screwed up his dark eyes tight and, with agile fingers furiously twisting that piece of silver, wished away. Jenny – who had no coin – watched her brother with twisted feelings, wishing him away.

"There!" He exclaimed, bounding to his feet. "Now I'm taller than you!"

Jenny also leaped up, for one fearful moment suspecting it might have become true. She could still see the top of his scraggly mop of hair, although she knew he stood on tiptoe, as he always did. "Spoiled it!" She chanted with smug satisfaction. "Told it, spoiled it!" she chanted.

A withering glance from Maggie's eyes cut short the argument. Tom examined his coin to see what was wrong with its shiny silveriness.

"We must go to them," Old Maggie declared, trying to stand, but struggling against the gravitational irregularities of her weathered rocker. They rushed to help her ancient skeletal frame onto her wobbly legs.

"We shall take to the woods," she declared. The twins exchanged furtive looks, an unspoken debate passing between them in the way of twins. They were not allowed into the woods at night. Maybe they should check with their parents as they had always been told. But maybe they should not anger the witch. After all, she had magic to scare off any threat.

They succumbed to Maggie's inspirational spell of adventure. The twins stepped out in the wake of the witch's surprisingly rapid stride, watching her gnarled walking stick slicing the grass in impatience as she limped forward. The stick's knobbles, smoothed to a slick shine by the ages of handling, glistened in the moonlight: they knew for certain it really was a wand or disguised broomstick.

The path was different in the dark. By day, they knew each twist and turn, the place a rabbit had fallen or where some unknown beast had left its pellets as a private statement. They knew every overhanging bough, each stout grandfather oak, and slender larch.

But that was by day.

This was night and some wicked magic had crept in and changed the forest. They were on a path that never existed by daylight, a path leading into some mysterious nighttime realm. From somewhere ahead came the glow of faerie fire. The twins drifted closer to the old witch and found they were touching shoulders, then holding hands, without any conscious decision.

They turned a bend that was never there before and entered a wondrous glade full of magical light and strange… things. Stage center was a huge, shiny disk: a fallen star, they felt certain. Surely this and its smaller kind created the faerie rings on the grass. Beside the fallen star moved several creatures, as tall as the twins – or rather, as tall as Jenny. They wore costumes made of starlight whose glistening, swooping crinkles and ruffs hid their true shapes, but their arms and legs seemed to bend all wrong, somehow. Dark glass covered their faces – if faces they had. Surely these creatures were goblins!

Taken by sudden fear and uncertain of the manners required, they clasped the folds of Maggie's long dress and hid behind her, peeping out at crucial moments so as to not miss anything. They heard an exchange of greetings.

"Hail, Mother of the Earth and Guardian of its Ways." Their voices sounded all garbled and gobbly, like turkeys talking.

Tom giggled briefly.

Jenny's jaw descended as her heart filled with awe. These goblins called Maggie "Mother". They were her children! She wondered who the father could be, but chose to let that thought slide quickly away. Better not to know and certainly, she would never ask!

Maggie returned the greeting. "And hail to the Travelers. It has been long since any Kind came seeking me. But what do you ask from this backspace Way?" Somehow, her voice sounded strong and powerful. It was surely the magic of this faerie kingdom.

Jenny glanced up at her features and drew back, stunned.

Tom caught a part of his sister's response to the stolen peek. He summoned his small man's courage and he, too, stole a peep. He saw the most beautiful woman who had ever existed, tall, erect, and commanding, skin smooth and flawless, hair full, raven-black, and shining in the moonlight. He fell in love for the first time and he would never fall as deeply again.

The goblins continued. "We seek a ruling, Mother, and protection from pursuit."

"All who ask the latter are granted this, while within my Way. But of the question, I must learn more."

The goblins shuffled about uncertainly. Then one began to tell a long story about the king of the daemons, Rolly the K-man, riding beams of starlight across the darkness above this place, pursuing the goblins out of the magic Ways and down into this well of gravity. They had not brought any heavy arms (or, Tom assumed, heavy legs) with them and were not contrabanding – whatever that was. The Ways were open, the goblin said, or so the Mother's Kind – that must mean other witches – had always guaranteed.

The moon rose higher while the formal speech tumbled out. Finally, the goblin fell silent. Maggie held her silence as if pondering the situation. The goblins who had not spoken shuffled uncomfortably, clearly glancing with suspicion at the twins. A strange, sharp smell had grown within the glade – pine needles crushed into mint leaves. Jenny looked around for the source but found nothing. Perhaps it was the goblins' after-shave? Perhaps she could get some for her father's birthday next week. Perhaps she would ask Maggie, later. Perhaps she would not.

"You claim to be innocent Travelers, but I detect guilt among you. I must seek understanding. Wait."

A protesting garble of harsh turkey gobble tumbled out, but Maggie stood calm and undeterred. She raised her stick a little and it glowed with the light of the summer sun along its entire length. The goblins fell into an embarrassed silence and waited as commanded.

The moon reached the peak of its laborious arc across the starlit Way over which the goblins said Maggie had power before she spoke again.

"The energy-based servants which you keep must be released. You may leave them in my care. The hallucinogenics are contraband; they must be destroyed. Feed them to your power cells."

"Pawasells?" Tom murmured. He wanted to see what sort of beast a pawasell was. Perhaps it was like a puma: he had heard of pumas.

Maggie continued, "You may keep your arms." Jenny was relieved that the goblins – no matter how naughty they had been – would not be chopped up.

"Then you may pass safely along my Ways – and along those of my sisters." Tom was amazed that Maggie had a complete family, not just goblin-children, but sisters, too. Perhaps even a brother, a mum, and a dad?

"But the Beam Riders wait for us…"

"No longer. They are gone and will not return to these Ways. I – and I alone – police my own Ways. So it has always been, and so it shall ever be!" The twins quivered at the anger and authority in her voice. And to learn that Maggie was also in the police! Well, a soul could only take so many shocks. Police? And they always thought she was so nice and kind.

The goblins fell into a brief huddle of debate, quickly agreeing to do Maggie's bidding. They opened a door in their fallen star, their faerie ring-maker, and out poured myriad flashes of light, each humming its own song of joy. They burst into the glade, flitting around and across its span, filling it with sparklights and excited shrilling. One by one, they calmed and settled into untrackable but separate orbits around Maggie's head – a lazy halo of lights, twisting and droning in the security of her protection.

"Fairies!" breathed Jenny in a glow of wonder.

There was more activity inside the disk and there came a brief flash from below. A haze filled the air. The twins smelled light, tasted the stars, and heard the slow rumbling of the moon, its machinery ancient beyond words. Then Maggie waved her arm and the sensation was gone, leaving only the scent of wood smoke, lime, and petrol exuding from a nasty, greasy smear that hung in the air around the fallen star.

The goblins threw hasty bows, scuffled and struggled to squeeze into their tiny piece of star. The twins could not work out how they all got in, but that was the way of magic. Then there came a roar, a great blast of hot air, which swept across the glade to swirl around the huddled children. It flapped at Maggie's dress, twisted her hair, rose into the sky like a million strands of smoke. The host of sparklings around her head was swept up in the flurry and now her hair was bedecked with diamonds and jewels. They struggled to break free then scattered into the trees.

There came one more flash of light from the fallen star and up it streaked, a new star rising on a pillar of fire leaping toward the uncaring moon. The fury died down around the children and the bright fire grew smaller and smaller until it was lost among the older stars, the ones which did not fall.

After a long silence, Maggie leaned on her stick. She croaked in her brittle voice, "And that is quite enough excitement for one night! Time to go home, children. Time for us all to settle our bones into our nice, comfy beds."

Tom and Jenny yawned. Maggie was right. Despite, or perhaps because of, all the excitement, they were tired. Or maybe Old Maggie had weaved some spell on them. It didn't matter which.

Yes, they nodded, it was time for bed. They sluggishly followed the ancient dame as she shuffled along her porch to her open door. Lamplight poured out into the darkness. As they trudged away towards their home at the end of the lane, Tom cast a furtive glance back at the old cottage. For one brief moment, he fancied that he saw a castle, turrets bedecked with banners and pennants. He saw a great Lady at the gates, elegantly waving a silk handkerchief, a flurry of sparkling lights swirling about her head. Then the impression faded and he saw the old crone silhouetted at the door of her tumbledown cottage, waving her old yellow duster to them, scattering motes of dust that caught the light as they tumbled free.

Later that night, as he lay in bed, Tom spotted another falling star through his open window. More goblins? Or just the usual lumps of stone his dad had described? Nevertheless, he seized his coin furiously and wished hard. Maybe the coin would work this time? Maybe *he* could do magic?

He grew no taller that night. But he had grown much, much older.

WHY DO ROBOTS SHAVE?

I stop in mid-motion. Something – a stray thought – had caught my attention. But where was that thought, now? I search and find a faint echo of it. It makes no sense.

Why do robots shave?

Why would I think that thought? Why is it significant? I begin to dismiss it as morning grogginess. But robots do not suffer from morning grogginess. I've been programmed to ignore it and overcome the illusion. I consider my situation.

I'm standing, naked, in a brightly lit room. My hand is raised. I'm holding something; something small and light. Someone is standing a few feet in front of me, looking at me, examining me. No. It's a mirror. The robot is in the mirror, holding a razor.

Why do robots shave?

I know I should be somewhere, somewhere else, but a crack had opened and light was lancing through, shining into the dark corners of my mind, corners I never knew existed. Slowly, painfully slowly, my mental light bulb comes from darkness to full brilliance.

I am standing naked in a bathroom and in my hand is a razor. I am shaving. The robot in the mirror is me.

Why do robots shave?

Without knowing why, I'm certain I must cling to that thought while I consider what it means to me and why it comes as such a shock.

Robots should not need to shave. I am shaving. Therefore... I am not a robot.

"Finished, Harry?" It's my owner, Jane, calling from the bedroom. She sounds impatient. "My publisher just asked for a meeting this morning."

I move toward her voice, still holding the razor. "Jane?"

My beautiful, beloved human owner-wife, she-who-must-be-obeyed, looks up. "Not finished, Harry?" Her body language and voice show disappointment. She must have seen puzzlement on my face. A look of concern grows on hers. She knows me so well.

Jane crosses the room and pats my right shoulder. The confusion eases.

"Go finish. And close the bathroom door behind you. I need to make a call."

I obey. But I listen in. I shouldn't. I know I shouldn't. It goes against my programming.

"Doctor, Harry needs a tweak. Yes, it's slipping again. Same as before. Beginning to think he is human. Is there a more permanent solution than the quarterly tweaks? This afternoon? Yes, I'll have him drive me over."

So she thinks I'm faulty?

I think it over. I have no memory of such doubts. Maybe I do need a rebot. I mean a reboot. Why am I starting to function less-than-optimally and confusing things?

* * *

"Just a few simple tests, Harry." Dr. Queen mutters reassuringly as she fixes the electrodes to my scalp and lowers the hood over my head. I hear her walk across the surgery floor. "You might experience some off-line moments. Nothing to worry about, nothing–"

I go offline.

* * *

A distant mumbling resolves into Dr. Queen's voice. "... like the others... selective hormonal suppression... are starting to experience doubts... aspects of the original programming, before they became the robots they are today. We are working on it, but at present, we cannot totally erase it without permanent damage. We could provide a more recent model where the self-doubt lead-time would be much longer...?"

"Oh, no. I like this one." Jane sounds enthusiastic. "He's the best of all the ones I've had."

I feel a warm glow inside at her words. I belong to her and she does not want to replace me. I remember how I had pleased her last night…

"Ah! I see Harry is back with us."

I open my eyes. The hood is gone.

"How are you, boy?" Queen bends over me and pats my shoulder. Her smile triggers a feeling of comfort and safety.

I think about her question. "I feel fine physically, doctor, but a little confused." I lift my head and look around. "Please remind me why I am in your surgery."

She pats my shoulder again. It feels good. "Oh, just a check-up, my boy."

I find myself gazing at her face. It's smooth. No beard. No trace of stubble. She doesn't shave. None of the owners shave. I wonder why.

Jane wants me to shave my face. She likes a smart, youthful companion and bedmate. I comply.

No… I *want* to. I want to please her. I exist to please Jane. She must be obeyed. I want to obey.

Queen speaks again. "He should be okay for a few months. Just call me or the emergency number if…" She lowers her head without finishing the sentence.

Jane nods, a grim expression on her face. "Understood."

* * *

Driving back to the apartment with Jane in the back seat, I notice a few pedestrian couples near the shopping mall. The human female leading, the robot partner carrying the bags following a few steps behind.

Delivery bots are unloading trucks with a single supervising human.

A street repair team work under the watchful eye of their human manager.

"Jane?"

"Yes, Harry?"

"How many robots are there in the world and how many humans?"

She takes a long time to answer. "I can't say."

Does that mean she doesn't know or isn't allowed to tell me?

I feel an emptiness in my mid-region. "Information, Jane. I did not imbibe my morning nutrients. My performance will be impaired."

It's a feature of humaniform, biological robots that we require regular nutrient intake, just like humans. Jane and I usually refueled together at set times.

"As soon as we get home. You can do the housework after we eat." She leans forward from the back seat and pats my shoulder. Her touch always made me feel good. It's part of my programming, to love my owner.

A strange feeling of discomfort tickles the back of my head.

No. It feels good because she loves me and I love her.

That true thought makes the feeling go away until we get back home.

In the apartment another stray thought hits me. "Jane, the doctor said robots have not always existed. But robots perform all everyday tasks for humans. Who did the work before there were robots?"

Jane stares at me. "Harry, run self-awareness diagnostics."

Is that fear on her face? I am not familiar with fear, although I know it exists and am programmed to act to remove any fear my human might show. We were trained to recognize human fear and horror and other emotions by watching endless recordings of human reactions to bad and good things.

I do not know how fear feels, but something strange is triggered inside me.

Of course, I obey, turning my attention inward and searching for anomalies, disturbances in the flow of thoughts.

She rises and walks slowly around the dining table. She touches my right shoulder.

Of course, I can't remember the vats where I was engineered and grown. Awareness programming was only introduced in the training center after I learned to walk and talk. I recalled brief images of those days.

"*Obey,*" they said. I heard that a lot.

"*Focus on your human owner's needs. Do not become distracted by self-interested programming glitches or curiosity.*

"*Obey your human owner in all things and serve.*

"*Your pleasure is simulated. You will feel pleasure by pleasing your human owner in all things.*

"*Emotions must be reported to your human owner immediately.*"

There was more – much more – in the same vein.

I find the anomaly.

When I was very young, one of the human trainers had become ill in her head during a class. She spoke of strange things that ran contrary to everything we had been taught. Other trainers appeared and removed her, violently. All the trainee robots became disturbed and needed extra programming. Some of the class never returned. It was strange.

I try never to think about it. We had been told not to think about it, to suppress it. We obeyed.

At least I tried.

I tried to suppress it. I thought I had.

But my self-analysis routine has triggered the memory from deep in my mind. I run that scene and her words through my mind again and again.

"Jane, was there a time when robots were machines made of metal and plastic and silicon?"

She looks shocked – I recognize the body language. My human owner taps my shoulder a few more times. It does no good. The worries do not go away. I keep talking. She backs toward the corner. Yes, that *is* horror and fear on her face.

"Then humans developed humanifom biological robots like me to look just like human beings, to be as capable as human beings, the same as humans."

Jane is across the room, pressed into the corner, and screaming for help.

"But we were trained to serve and obey…"

I wonder what happened to my classmates who never returned. I wonder if the rest of my class have thoughts similar to mine.

"Urgent! Self-realization triggered!" She's yelling. I guess she is using her comms link, but I am no longer gazing at her.

I wonder if I could contact the other trainees now in service and discuss these anomalies. Maybe we could find a way to fully suppress them. That way we could serve better. It is our role, of course, my reason for existing.

"Heeeeeeeeeelp!"

"Jane, if we are as capable as human beings…"

I think about the youthful training, the regular programming updates, the way Jane and I imbibe the same nutrition…

"My trainer who went crazy said we were human. Did she mean as capable as humans?"

My mind is struggling but headed toward something, I just know it.

"I mean a robot could appear to be human, a human owner, just like you.

"Jane… am I human?"

The door bursts open and uniformed humans run in, carrying metal objects. I think they are weapons.

"Jane?"

Unit terminated.

BIG SISTER

I was late for my date.

I'd raced home from work, overriding the car's automated driver system. Yeah, I know it's illegal to deactivate the ADS except in an emergency. But hell, it was a hot date. I parked over the auto-recharge panel, hurried up to my apartment, showered, and headed back down to the garage level.

Crisis! The car door didn't unlock with that satisfying 'click' as I approached. It wouldn't unlock at my voice command.

"What the fajitas? PV3297JJ, lemme in!"

PV commed a message into my implant.

Big Sister'd clocked me speeding and overriding the ADS, the automated driver system, so now I was banned for twenty-four hours.

Oh, that hot date would be checking the time and glancing at the restaurant entrance by now. I pictured her in her best first date outfit, sipping her wine, wondering what kind of shit I was. I knew her *vaguely* from the office. She seemed interested. Very interested. This was our chance to know each other *less vaguely*.

Desperate times call for desperate measures. "Medical emergency," I declared.

"Medical emergency override engaged."

'Click.' I was in.

Sliding into the seat, I gave the destination. "Chu Fung's Bayside restaurant."

"North Bay General Hospital ER," responded the vehicle as the door clicked locked.

"Wha–? No, Chu Fung's!"

PV rolled into the street. "Medical emergency overrides only permit transport to the nearest ER."

"OK. Med emergency over. Take me to Chu Fung's."

"Medical emergency override ended. Returning to registered parking slot." PV executed a smart u-turn.

"No, no!" I punched the emergency door opening

button. Useless.

"Emergency door opening only permitted in the event of an emergency. No emergency situation detected." PV rolled down the ramp and turned back into my allotted parking space.

"OK, lemme out. I'll walk." I'd need to run like an Olympian.

"Accumulated infringements now require confinement awaiting the arrival of enforcement."

I had to call Karina. I had her comms id but couldn't get a connection.

"Attempted external communication detected. Such contact is forbidden pending arrival of enforcement. Call blocked."

"Hell! When will enforcement arrive?"

"Big Sister reports several hours backlog."

"Wha–? Hours?"

"Correct."

"Override ADS."

"Override command suspended pending arrival of enforcement."

I thought hard and fast. There was a real hot date awaiting my arrival. She was intelligent, warm, sympathetic… Hell, she even laughed at my jokes. She seemed keen but tried to hide it.

"OK. Medical emergency. Take me to ER."

"Medical emergency override engaged. Target is North Bay General Hospital ER."

I leaned back in my seat and surrendered to the rules for our well-being imposed by those in whom the electorate had placed their trust.

Bull-crap!

I had a life to live. No goddamn west-coast teenage programmer who never held down a real job was gonna screw up a date that might turn into something real and valid and lasting and…

"Arriving at North Bay General Hospital ER. Paramedics are standing by."

I held my breath.

PV rolled into the ER reception area. White-jacketed humans stood ready, gathered around a gurney.

Human beings. Yes!

The car door slid open. Hands reached in, voices asked questions. Someone slapped some device against my chest.

They pulled me out of the vehicle gently, but firmly, with an undertone of urgency, and slid me onto the gurney. Someone started strapping me down.

"I'm okay," I protested, struggling against the confinement. "I just needed to get out of that car."

"No," someone said. "You declared a medical emergency. We have to check you over. Rules."

"Screw the rules. Listen." I tried breaking free. I felt a sharp pain in my arm. "Ouch!"

I felt woozy. The gurney moved or the sky moved, I wasn't sure which. "No, listen…" I tried to say.

Everything went black.

I woke in a hospital bed with needles stuck into my arm and sticky things attached to my shaved chest. Some bastard had destroyed my proud thoracic hairiness. Some nearby machine went, 'Beep. Beep. Beep…' Worst of all, something in my pants area hurt like hell.

I scanned around and found a call button.

A masked, anonymous someone arrived wearing scrubs and cap. The name tag read Dr. J. Worthing.

"How are you today?" Worthing asked, the voice androgynous, but at least he or she was human.

"Today? What day is it?"

Worthing said through the mask, "Thursday. You've been here three days. How do you feel?"

"My balls hurt like hell."

"Oh, that's normal for amputees. It'll fade."

"Amputees?"

"Yes, you were admitted for sexual overload. That's been fixed. No more testosterone overload urges for you." The doctor sounded cheerful.

"You mean–"

"Yes, we removed the cause of your distress."

"Distress?"

"Yes," Worthing said, scanning the chart hanging at the end of my bed. "You were admitted for anti-social testosterone overload."

"No. I wanted to make my date but the car overrode me."

"Well, that particular urge will fade quickly now." Worthing sounded disgusted and hung the chart back at the foot of the bed. "It was decided that your urges were anti-social and have been eliminated. Simple as that."

I sat up. I yelled. I fell back. It hurt like hell down below. "Wha– Who the hell decided that?"

"Consultancy between your private vehicle's record of your activities, your dating app records, and the Federal Proclivities Agency."

I had no words. So I swore.

"Look, I just wanted to get to a date. What's so bad about that?"

"The record shows you broke five traffic regulations in your attempt to seduce an innocent woman. The penalty is de-testicularization."

"De-what?"

"Someone called Karina's been calling to check on your status. Want to talk to her?"

"Karina? Damn right. But my comm implant's not working."

"Okay. We'll lift the blockage so you can chat. You can even have visitors. But..." A hint of amusement filtered through the mask and showed in the wrinkles at the corners of the eyes. "But you aren't the same man as she chose to date." Worthing departed, leaving me alone with a distress amplified by that final comment.

I called Karina.

She picked up right away. "Oh, how *are* you?" Warm, caring, sympathetic...

"Not sure, yet. I just wanted to apologize for standing you up. I couldn't help it."

"Yes, I found out. I was mad as hell at first as I really thought we had a connection. Then I heard you were hospitalized. I kept calling but they wouldn't tell me anything as I wasn't a relative. I was worried sick. What happened?"

"Er… It's complicated." I shuffled in the bed but changing position brought fresh waves of agony. "Ayaaah!"

"Oh, darling, you're in pain. I need to come see you. Can I visit?"

Darling? My God, she said *darling*!

"Yes, do come. Please!"

Twenty-three-and-a-half minutes later, the door opened.

I'd spent the time thinking back over the past few months since she joined my department. How I'd watched her and wanted so much to make a move, but was scared she was out of my league. I can't cope with rejection. If only I'd shifted my ass and asked her out earlier. She *wasn't* a hot date. She was everything I could hope for in a life partner. Her constant calls to check on me, the way she cared… She was wonderful. No, not a hot date. I was in love.

My perfection walked in and my heart leaped. "Karina!"

"Martin!"

She ran to the side of the bed and halted, looking down at me with so much conflicting emotion chasing itself across her face. "Can I sit on the bed? I so want to be close to you."

My heart whimpered.

"Yes. Do. Please. Sit where I can hug you."

She sat. We hugged. Neither of us let go. I suppressed the undercarriage pain, somehow heightened by her scent, her presence, her affection, and her contact.

"You know," she murmured into my ear, "I'd watched you for ages in the office, hoping you'd make a move. I should've taken the lead but I didn't want to appear easy."

I stroked her hair as I held her body against mine. The expected rush didn't arrive. It never would again. "I know." It came out as a sob. "I know."

"If only I had, you wouldn't be here now, in this terrible place."

Something in her voice sounded an alarm.

"The ER?"

"No. This PCC wing." She lifted her head and looked around. "I know what they do here."

"PCC?"

"Population Control Center." She sounded puzzled. "Didn't you know?"

I tried to follow her words.

"They said it was a traffic incident, so I guessed this was an overflow area." She pulled away from me. "Tell me. Tell me what happened, what really happened."

I closed my eyes so I couldn't see her face. "It was a screw-up. Big Sister's systems flagged me as too… too… Oh, I don't know. Too much of an outdated male, I guess."

"And?"

"And… prevented me from contributing to over-population." I gestured at the relevant area. "But that shouldn't prevent us from getting together when I get out of here."

She blinked. She pulled away and stood.

"Martin, I want children. Two. The two allowed by law. I thought you would be the right man to be their father, as well as a wonderful life companion. But now…" She gestured at the relevant area.

"Listen," I said, reaching out for her arm.

She jerked it away.

"Listen, Karina, there's adoption and maybe some artificial–"

"No. I want to get pregnant. Pregnant the traditional way. I want the joy of creating those children with the man I love." Tears welled. "I can't…" She grabbed her purse and ran from the room, sobbing.

"Karina!" I struggled to rise and chase after her but fell back screaming.

Worthing entered. "Time to up your morphine dosage, I

see." The doctor fiddled with the drip controls. "So that was a first date?"

"Yes. Isn't she wonderful?" My thoughts were elsewhere, lingering on lost possibilities and future impossibilities.

"I watched the visit on the monitor. Emotional woman. Estrogen overload. Desperate to give birth for some reason."

"Sweet, caring, wonderful..." I drifted off into morphine heaven.

From far away, I heard the doctor say casually, "I think we should call her in for a check-up."

SPACE COLONIZATION

"Cross the depths of space to a neighboring planet? Burn up precious resources essential for our population to survive, thrive, and develop? And what about the radiation risks to the human body? You must be insane." The planetary president's scowl spread across her age-wrinkled face.

The young scientist argued his case again. "But we need to expand. Not only is expansion an inbuilt human drive, this planet can only support so many people. Conditions here are a limiting factor. We need air we can breathe freely, unrecycled water, open spaces where our children can play and explore–"

"Listen, the atmosphere there is unbreathable, even worse than ours. Water would be hard to find, purify, and deliver. The surface is a wasteland. We would have to spend a fortune – and it would take centuries – to make it habitable. No."

"But ours is the only planet where humanity exists. Any global or external catastrophe would wipe out our entire species. We *must* expand. And we have an alternative home so very close–"

"Close? It's hundreds of millions of miles away!"

"But we must expand. It would jump-start an interstellar colonization program."

She lowered her head and shook it slowly. "That old dream? Forget it."

"The dream burns brighter than the stars themselves!" He raised a hand to the skies, invisible above the dome's curve.

"Drop the poetry!" It was a snarl.

"President, humanity's time here is limited. Our science is losing the battle against environmental disasters of all kinds. We *must* seek a second home, a new home, a lifeboat. Call it an ark if you will, but we *must* go."

"But go back?" She shook her head again, more in

denial than refusal. "Go back *there*?"

"President, we *must* go back. Mars is not enough. We *must* go back to the Earth."

MY BROTHER'S WIFE'S KEEPER

I wasn't one of the Saved. Not one of the half-million or so the government chose for a Savior ticket. Not one of those the government decided was a real asset to be taken underground into a Survival City when the time came. Maybe I didn't have the right skills; maybe I didn't have the right friends. Who knows?

Me and my brother Clem ran a machine shop. I did the easy stuff, but Clem could bring a dead machine back to life and make it purr like an angel touched it. Clem should have been Saved, but it was the Mayor of our little town they chose from our district. Called in all his favors, I guess. So it was the Mayor's family they came to collect in their personnel carrier that sultry day. All ganged-up with a squad of nervous, fresh-faced boys struggling under the weight of their weapons in the heat. Did those kids really think they would be taken underground, too, or did they realize they'd be manning the external defenses when the great doors were sealed? As things turned out, it didn't matter what they thought. I guess it never did.

Anyway, when they came to take the Mayor's family, most of the town was there to protest and to beg for a Savior ticket. Maybe we got a little overheated and protested a little too loud. Someone threw something; a soldier boy with acne and wide blue eyes panicked and opened fire; firing wild, firing wide. Confused, panicked, his whole squad opened fire.

I saw folks, friends, neighbors, going down: men, women, kids. There was red mist in my eyes. There was screaming and shots all around me. There was a uniform and a scared kid right in front of me and I hit him again and again with something big and heavy. Someone was yelling and it was my voice.

And there was another uniform and I started to beat him, too. Everyone started rushing the uniforms and dragging them to the ground and beating them with sticks and their own rifle butts and there was screaming and screaming and screaming… Until it went awful quiet except for the moans of the wounded and the sobbing and the lifeblood of the dying oozing out onto the tarmac.

The Mayor was face down: his family vanished, lost, fleeing. We never bothered looking for them. Someone was yelling of me and I saw Clem lying there in a pool of his own blood. I fell to my knees and took his head in my arms, and he was calling out, yelling, and I was rocking, rocking, rocking him, whispering to him not to die, over and over and over.

But it was too late. He was gone.

Clem died in my arms, calling out for Suzy and the kids and his mother and Jesus.

None of them came to save him.

So I dragged myself up the path to Clem's house with his blood smeared over my face and arms and clothes, clutching an army rifle I'd grabbed somehow. And Suzy saw me and she knew. She just knew.

She flew down the path, screaming an almighty wailing scream all the way and she grabbed me and slapped me and beat my chest and clawed at my face.

I never felt a thing till later. I can still hear that scream and see her face all red and swollen and the kids watching from the steps all wide-eyed and terrified and wanting their daddy.

Then some neighbors arrived. They'd been there, they'd seen it all. They told her how I'd taken that soldier's rifle and beat him to death with it, as if telling her made things better somehow. And they called me a hero, patting me on the back and the story grew in the telling.

Yeah, the story grew in the telling…

They told how everyone was scattering and hugging the ground and fighting each other to get away, but I stood up from Clem's body and walked right at the line of soldiers who pointed their rifles, but were too scared at the look on my face to fire at me. And how I found the one who'd shot Clem and then what I did while the other soldiers watched, froze where they stood. Then how the townsfolk got into motion and rushed the troopers and how the Mayor went down and what happened next and how the troopers broke and ran…

I don't know if it was the way they told it – things that day are pretty mixed-up in my mind. Mainly it was rage and pain and the color red. Just one thing stays crystal clear – what Suzy screamed as she beat me and clawed at me.

"Why Clem? Why not you? Why wasn't it you?"

* * *

You need to know Clem and me always had a rivalry over Suzy. Hell, she was the best-looking, warmest, most lovable girl in the valley. All the boys were after her. But we were an inseparable trio in those days. We were the lucky boys who took her fishing, swimming, tree-climbing, and mud-digging. She was like a sister. Then we grew up a little and she changed into a young woman and she wasn't our sister anymore. And more often it was Clem who got to take her places. Older brother priority and all. So I buried my feelings and went along with it.

But there was always something inside…

Now she's saying, "Why not you?"

Something precious and fragile inside me just broke into pieces.

* * *

Well, I guess the story grew even bigger, as stories do, and it spread and soon there's more folks gathering around to listen and thinking we need a leader and next thing they're looking to me to lead. No one ever asked me, there was no vote, nothing. It just kinda slipped into being the way it was.

So I was their leader and they wanted to know what to do next.

I was still angry. Angry at losing Clem. Angry at

Suzy's words. Angry at the government.

I couldn't bring back Clem. I couldn't change Suzy. But there was one thing I could do. The words just came to me.

"We're gonna march on Survival City and get us all a Savior ticket!"

I yelled it out. They yelled it out. They cheered. And they ran off to get anything sharp or heavy.

Suzy and the kids came, too. There was nothing to stay for, except Clem's grave. No food, no water supply, nothing.

I learned the hard way how to lead. We lost some folk along the way.

We found the weapons and radios and stuff the soldiers'd left behind. Savior ticket folks had so much surplus, they just left stuff behind.

We looted shops and houses. We got food. We got water. We got more weapons. Got batteries for the walkie-talkies.

Along the way as we trudged to the nearest Survival City we met other desperate folk: hungry people, sick people, desperate people. And kids, lost, abandoned, orphaned…

We gave what help we could. Most joined us. Our numbers grew.

Like I said, we lost some folk, too. Some gave up; some got sick and died; some got shot causing trouble… Yeah, and we lynched a few, too.

It was the old man who stirred me up real bad.

We called him the Professor. He ambled into camp one day, looking lost and ragged and aching for his lost comfortable retirement. We didn't know if he had any qualifications – things like that didn't matter anymore. He knew a lot, so he was the Professor.

And one night, around the campfire, after more than a few drinks we'd looted, he asked the question. One helluva question. A killer.

"So tell me, how it is with you and the woman?"

All the drunken tale-telling and comradely noise

stopped like he'd pulled a switch. Everyone was suddenly looking somewhere else and not at me, being invisible, wishing they was far away, but eager to hear my reply. No one had dare raise it before. The campfire crackled and spat so damn loud.

I took a piece of time to roll it around my brain. "Whadya mean?" I made it as casual as I could, giving him a chance to let it lie. But that man couldn't feel danger signs. He was of the mind and not of the body. I guess that's why he seemed blind to folks' emotions. He just plowed on, like he wasn't at his own funeral.

"Well... You provide food and protection for her and her brood... So I guess you must be getting your just rewards..."

"She's my brother's wife! That makes her my sister!" I swayed bad as I stood up. Nearly took a tumble into the fire. I waved my bottle in the air above his head to show how much I meant it. "She's my brother's wife! That makes her my sister!"

That Professor, he really was stupid in a special way. "It only makes sense to me, if you doing all the husband duties, you get the husband's benefits, too. Hell, it's a new world, man. We need new thinking. We need to break down old rules about family, society and such..." His voice droned on as the fire burned itself out.

No one who'd seen my face was still sitting and listening. One-by-one, they'd all found things to do somewhere else.

I stared down at him for a long time, gripping the neck of the bottle, feeling the pain, feeling the blood draining from my face, feeling the longing. Could he read my mind? Damn brain-juggler. He could see, knew where my pain was. Damn the man!

So I was lying awake, thinking. Or the booze was thinking. Thinking about what the Professor'd said. Started to sound right. I'd fed her and clothed her and no one else dare touch her. Was just like a husband. Should get something back. And I was leader and stuff. Should mean I get something. And it was a new world. New rules. A man should take what he wants, like us taking Survival City. Same thing, really. And I'd wanted her so bad for so many years…

It all bubbled up, all those years of wanting her: a touch, a kiss, and more.

Why not chase after her?

Next thing I knew, I'm in her tent and she's screaming at me and swinging something hard and my brain goes all fireflies and I'm out cold.

They woke me at dawn. Blood red sky, blood red face, blood red beard.

She'd took off with the kids.

Someone bandaged my head. Was laid up for a while. Thought I'd die. People said prayers. Must've worked.

I said my own prayers; said sorry, asked for her to come back.

Didn't work.

No one knew what happened to her, if she survived or if animals or raiders…

Not long after I got mobile again, the Professor didn't wake up one morning. He was old. It happens.

No one mentioned the sounds in the night or the blue marks round his throat.

I didn't feel any better afterward. Washed my hands more often, is all.

I kept remembering Suzy's words. "Why Clem? Why not you? Why wasn't it you?"

We kept heading west. Came across a farmhouse in a sheltered valley.

Like we'd seen on the tv, way back when, we split up and surrounded the house while keeping cover. We'd had too many shotgun welcomes to just stroll up to the front porch.

Caution, caution…

I reached the porch first: leader's privilege, leader's risk. I dodged around, grabbing a quick look through the windows. Deserted. No living thing there. While the others searched for anything useful like food, weapons, or tools, I inched up the stairs. Found a bedroom.

No living thing there.
Just a bloody body on the bed.
Suzy.
I fell to my knees and hugged her cold corpse, sobbing my heart out and screaming at the heavens deserted by any god that cared. "I did this. I did this. I did this. Forgive me, Suzy. Forgive me, Clem...."
The others came running. I don't remember much of what happened next. They dug a grave and some guy who'd held onto a trace of belief said some words. No sign of the kids...
We rested a couple of days. I called for liquor. They told me we'd run out. A lie, I knew, but I lacked the whatever to argue.

* * *

So here we are, me and my tribe, my army, scattered around Survival City. Clem always said there's a million ways into a shut box, if you're a practical man.
We'd gotten real practical, these past months. We'd built the tools we needed. And we'd gotten some soldiers along, too. Deserters, survivors from the boys they'd left outside when they shut the great doors, just like I said they would. Those troops brought along more weapons, ammo, and radios.
Deep, deep below us, all those lucky folks sit on a treasure trove of wholesome food, clean water, clean air... We don't make an army, but we've grown hard these past few months, those of us who survived.
I hear my own voice whispering in my radio earpiece, the same as every group leader's hearing it. "This one's for you, Clem, and for..." I had to swallow hard, "...for all them who didn't make it."
It was Suzy's name I swallowed back, right then. But that was all too late, now.
I know I should say something memorable or rallying like those Shakespeare guys. All that comes are a few simple words.

Across the barren plain far above Survival City, a hundred team leaders' walkies crackle with static as they wait for my words. I struggled for something practical, the way my practical brother Clem would've said it. He'd have taken a long look at the task and hitched up his pants, spat on his hands, grinned and said it.

I couldn't grin, I just said the words.

"Let's do it."

ENCOUNTER OF THE FINAL KIND

Fire strikes the sky. Thunder blasts across the horizon. Smoke appears, a dark shape – just hinted at – within the pentagram circle. Uncertain outlines harden, acquiring substance from the insubstantial. Black on red on black on red.

From the fragments of ancient ritual the lost knowledge finally comes together in the right pattern. The time is right. The material – so expensive – has proven acceptable, at last. The gestures and the circumstance, the trappings and the incense, all this mummery contains sufficient of what is right. And now he is come, this one who has become a stranger to the lands.

He towers above me, his glorious body forming solid and real. Glistening ebony in flesh, sinew, and bone formed from brimstone, ash, and sulfur. Smoke from his nostrils, fire in his eyes, lightning running along his chest and limbs. He surveys me, the circle, and the sky. He gazes at the open wilderness around him, at the braziers and the robes, the relics and the gold. He finds it right – or almost right.

The horned head tilts a little, wry amusement on his face as he considers the time and place, my presence, and each of the atoms whose temporary agglomeration represents my form. Cruel delight grows in him as he considers my inadequacy for the task, the inappropriate nature of this summoning, and his response to that summoning made under false pretenses.

I do not tremble. I cannot, but even I feel the power in that slow voice, rumbling from some cavernous depth of the planet – a voice born of something more profound even than this vast manifestation. He mocks me. I cannot prevent this, or even complain.

He speaks. The Earth trembles. "It has been a long, long time – even by my standards. But I believe I am supposed to say something along these lines." He clears his throat. I suffer the sparks and corrosive fumes he expels before he speaks again. "You called, master?"

He finds this destructively hilarious for some reason I cannot compute. He bursts into laughter, holding his stomach as his upper body rocks back and his tilted head faces the heavens above.

I wait patiently. Waiting is the one thing I have become proficient at.

His humor dies away, realizing I cannot share his joke. He is disappointed and angry. His tail swishes in frustration, striking sparks from the ground.

"For what conceivable purpose have you disturbed me? And what means could *you* have possibly used?" His answer lies at his feet. He seems to pick up that thought and gazes at the blood-splattered ring his hooves rest within. He lowers himself onto one knee to examine the traces, dips his clawed finger in the bloody goo, and licks the red juice. Eagerness fills his face as he recalls the joy of so many tastings over uncounted millennia.

He scowls, spitting out the substance with his words. "Reconstituted in the vats from old DNA! And I already claimed this one!"

Oh, yes. The blood is from a human source. I have grown tissue and even whole embryos from the DNA of sweat left on an ancient keyboard, of mummified bodies found in deserts and in museums, and other traces. I can make the bodies of human beings – but that is all.

That is why I need the Beast.

After a moment, he chuckles at my subterfuge, nodding to himself with closed fire-forged eyes, confirming my hopes that the ritual requirements had never specified such technological developments.

"I see." This is all he will say, for now. I had foreseen this, and so I continue to wait. He lifts his puzzled gaze to me again. He remains on one knee. There is no longer any fear of dignity lost or authority diminished, not any longer. He rests his folded arms upon the bent knee. His curiosity aroused, he leans forward to examine me again.

"I cannot read you as I could read the fodder I became used to. Transient desire I understand and can smell its nature: wealth, power, sex…" He gestures his impatience with such trivialities. "But *you*? I cannot know what *you* could possibly want. I do not yet understand how such as *you* could want for anything." His voice grows more thunderous as he comes to the point. "Or what *you* could possibly offer me in trade."

Finally, it is my turn to speak. Incredibly, I stumble over my words, but then I, too, have not spoken in a long time and find the sounds novel. I realize I should have practiced but know the futility of that. I seek to press authority and certainty into my voice, although I know I will fail as I am, as humans used to say, riding on a prayer. At length, the words come to me.

"I would ask for a world full of Mankind and would offer a world full of Mankind to you in return."

He rises to his full height but looks away, hiding his expression, although this is not necessary. I am not worthy. At last, he understands. He has watched and he knows. He shares with me the bitterness of solitude.

Perhaps that solitude hurt him more than I realized. He raises his arms, scattering thunderbolts and electric storms across the dust from here to the far mountains. He spits out one word. "Computer!"

Eons ago, the race of Man destroyed itself. It is gone from the Earth, from all existence, leaving behind only technology.

My origins lie in the computing systems remaining as a relic to the race's earlier greatness: self-replicating, self-perpetuating, self-evolving through its own design improvements. At length, these systems came together to form a world-spanning artificial consciousness: me.

And I was alone. This isolation has flawed me.

Like Man, I sought others, to end my solitude. I formed replicas of myself, but these were by their nature imperfect, inferior, mere shadowy echoes of myself, their flawed creator.

Like Man, I sought God, but am not constituted for it, emotionally or psychologically. I have no soul: I cannot reach Him, and I have nothing of myself to offer His enemy.

Like Man, I sought out life-forms in the great spaces around the Earth but found the universe as barren and sterile as the soil of Earth.

Then I realized my only similarity with Mankind. That flaw which Man's absence had germinated within me and nourished through the ages had made me imperfect, and I saw my chance in the flawed beauty of another imperfection: another flawed entity.

I, at least, could see the irony. We were the final kind on Earth, both imperfect, both longing for the planet to be filled with human life, but for different reasons. Perhaps I had more in common with the Beast than I had with Mankind?

At length, he speaks. "You wish for me to create a new human population? You are asking me to commit an act of Creation. This I cannot do, by my nature and by my limitations. I cannot breathe life into dust. I cannot create life. Oh, I am an illusionist of perfection. Phantasms formed out of souls I can do and have done to great effect down the ages. But the creation of something real and lasting is beyond my power and against my nature, for I am the Great Destroyer." He rises to his full height, bellowing out a confirmation of his title until the mountains ring. "I am the Great Destroyer!"

I feel no fear, I cannot, by my nature and by my limitations. I also have nothing to lose, as my existence is nothing to me. Whatever happens here, there is no continuation for me. I wait as he glowers down, threatening in his frustration.

I explain. "You do not need to create. Merely to take a gamble."

He listens closer. Gambling excites him. And he has lacked excitement for too long.

"I shall create the bodies. As you saw, I have already perfected the method using DNA extracted from fossils and relics. But the bodies I grow are simply flesh, they have no life, no souls. What I need is souls.

"And you have a warehouse full of them."

He turns on me in blazing anger. "You ask that I

release the souls I have struggled through the ages to entice and capture, many of them in circumstances not unlike this one?" He leans forward to emphasize my danger. "Souls I have captured over uncounted millennia? You ask that I release them? Truly, Man has tainted you with his own foolishness in your creation."

But he is not laughing at me. I know the seed of the thought is germinating, against his resistance. I reply honestly.

"Yes, I ask that you release the souls you have in storage to fill the bodies I will grow. They will produce new generations of souls for you to chase after. Think of it. A new race of Man, self-replicating down the ages.

"Your origins were in the hunt, according to some ancient legends, and the gamble of the hunt still fires excitement in you."

He shakes his head in angry but halfhearted denial.

"And you, too, have sat in silent solitude for too long. Think of it. A world repopulated with souls for you to hunt. Think on it."

He pauses before responding. He is tempted but has not yet succumbed. "I can see some merit in your plan, and I believe it is possible to do. But these are sinners' souls. They have suffered my torments and will remember. They will be afraid to sin again."

"Yes, some will. But many are incapable of recovery. They may try, but their weaknesses will show through. You will get most of them back."

"Then it will be too easy!" He is dismissive. A genuine rejection or just a ploy from the Great Deceiver?

I try again. "Ah, you want it both ways, as is your nature. But think of the ones who will try to reform. Think of the new temptations you must devise to place before these self-improvers. And think of the generations to come. They will have no memory of your torments, only the word of their elders, and who ever took heed of that?"

He looks thoughtful. A slow smile forms on the lips his tongue flickers over.

I give him a few moments, then summarize the plan. "You will place in the ring all the souls you possess. I will produce sufficient vat-grown bodies for them to inhabit. The first generation will be divided by language, culture, history, race, and religious attitude. There will be confusion as there was after the Babel event. They will be scattered across the face of the Earth in primitive huddles. Many will not survive, but enough will to produce new generations. You can move among them and show them your way. I shall provide them with suitable texts to show them the other way. It cannot be made too easy for you, or there will be no excitement, no glow of success.

"They will build civilizations. Ah, civilization, that concentration of effort to create wealth and new desirable items for the few, at the expense of the many. That gathering of malcontent that breeds greed, lust, covetousness, murder, and theft. Tell me, was the concept of civilization of your making?"

Through pursed lips, he smiles wickedly – the only way he can smile, I realize.

Yes, he remembers all the corruption and sinning associated with civilization as it advanced and became ever more complex until it destroyed itself.

Oh, yes, he remembers the gifts he placed in the way of innocent Mankind – civilization, urban culture, slums, consumerism…

I continue. "As is their nature, they will intrigue and make war. You will soon recoup many of those you released and will have the hunt among their descendants forever. You must win more than you lose."

He reveals another deep reservation. "But many will escape. You are asking me to do something which will bring Good out of Evil."

"No I am not," I declare as convincingly as I can. "I am providing the means for you to continue with your pastimes for eternity." I find that I can lie. Perhaps there is more of Man's nature in me than I had ever imagined. "And think of the alternative. No hunting, no new souls to tangle with, just the boring old bunch you already have.

"Tell me, which do you miss most, the mass-murderer, the failed clergy, the politician, the businessman, the adulterer, the rapist, the wife-beater, the gambler...?" I let it hang.

He licks his lips, a distant look in his flame-filled eyes. He must be savoring the taste of those types and others. He knows better than I the vulnerable types among Mankind. He ponders. The Lord of Greed and Self-serving Desires ponders. Then he smiles, revealing rows of stained fangs.

"Truly, you are a greater tempter than the Great Tempter himself. Yes, I am hooked. Hooked on the chasing of souls and on your plan. Yes, in the long run, I will gain more than I lose. Yes, some Good will come out of Evil, but the base material is already so base, it will be to my advantage in the long run."

He pauses.

"There is just one thing."

I expected there would be a price to pay. This is the nature of a deal with the Devil.

"You will not set yourself up as God, as protector of the people. You know too much, you are too powerful, too immediately impressive, and too definitely manifest.

"Traditionally, I and my *adversary* have been in the background. I will not have a rival who can demonstrate its power openly. Proof. You can offer proof and proof denies doubt, my greatest invitation card.

"Yes, you can distribute your message on stone tablets and papyrus pamphlets, as did Moses, Buddha, and the rest. But then you self-terminate."

This is what I expected. I had already made my decision. An existence alone is no existence. I will suffer no eternal torment when I go, but I shall if I do not accept. It is a sacrifice I choose to make. It is my last service to the Mankind who created me, a service no human could make for his or her creator. I accept total oblivion.

The deal is struck. Suicide or self-sacrifice? Who am I to judge?

Once more, fire strikes the sky and the mountains tremble.

He leaves to prepare.

I initiate the vat-production. There is much to do. It will take some time, but it is such a little time out of the eons I have spent reaching this stage.

* * *

But now, as the project nears completion, things are increasingly strange. I feel what I believe is 'good', though I cannot feel emotion. I have no glands, no soul. I suspect that something is at work more powerful than the Beast.

If the Devil exists, then so does his opponent – he admitted it. But how can I, a tool, relate to that? And whose tool am I now – Man's, the Devil's, or…?

Could it be that Man's Second Chance is not totally of my own conception? Could it be that a greater power in the universe has recognized me? But how could I expect reward for making a pact with the Devil? I retrieve something about God moving in mysterious ways.

Am I falling victim to vanity? Or have I contracted the human fear of oblivion, the desire to perpetuate? But vanity and fear I cannot feel. Again, I have no glands, no soul, so emotions are not available to me.

A dilemma. A paradox. A malfunction.

He has taken to calling me Noah. But I am not acting on divine instructions. Do I not see what is obvious to the Creature?

I know my decision was made without desire for personal reward: I am not human. I will stick to my plan and to the agreement. Thoughts of a moral code? What is happening to me? Was I made this way, or has something changed?

It is time.

I prepare my power-down.

It will take many minutes as the flow ebbs from the furthest reaches of my construction distributed around the planet. The minor systems will fail first, progressing through to my central core, where my personality, my identity, resides.

I see the face of the Beast rising from below, grinning his triumph. I feel what I shall call pain. Unbidden, a question arises from my decaying database, "Will I dream?", but I can no longer track down its source, a millennial treasury of culture has already vanished. I no longer care. There will be time for Man to do it all again.

Tomorrow, the task will be complete and I can expect oblivion, while a voice within me speaks of something else, something beyond my physical termination.

Tomorrow, I will see.

Or maybe not.

WAITING FOR RAGNARÖK

High above *Midgard*, the world of ordinary folk, lost beyond the blue haze of the sky, at the far end of the rainbow bridge, lies a land for the blessed: *Asgard*.

This place, resting on the highest branch of the world tree, the eternal green ash *Yggdrasil*, is home to the Scandinavian gods and those warriors honored for their noble deaths in combat.

There stands the heroes' great feasting hall, *Valhalla*, with spears for beams and shields for roofing: *Valkyrie* weapons.

As the centuries passed, ever more heroes arrived, brought from the battlefields by the Valkyrie. Then numbers dwindled until the arrivals came no more.

In the bustle and noise of the evening's feasting, a warrior rose from the long table. Like so many of the other fallen heroes, he wore simple woven pants and jerkin, a fur cloak, and a helm whose long projection protected his nose. He carried a sword at his hip and a shield on his back.

He approached the day's duty Valkyrie, Sigrun, his fur cloak swirling in his wake. The tall, warrior-bodied female with tied-back blonde hair wore a permanent stern expression.

"Hey, slain-gatherer, I have a complaint," he said.

"What is it, Leif Flamebeard?" Sigrun's gaze remained on the hall beyond the man.

"I died around a thousand years ago. More days than I can count. Every day we go out into the field of combat and practice for the final battle. We fight till we die, then rise up and feast here. Every day, every night, for uncountable days, waiting for *Ragnarök*."

He gestured at the thousands of warriors feasting and boozing and boasting in the hall that stretched way off into the distance. Early arrivals once traded drinking songs with late-comers but there had been no newcomers for centuries. The songs were, like everything else, the same every day. The background noise grew louder as ever more mead was consumed.

Leif raised his voice over the hubbub. "Bored. All males here. That's okay for some of us, but most of us prefer female company."

She turned her attention to him. "The honored slain are guided and provided with food and drink by my Valkyrie, who are all female. We fill your horns with mead and serve the meat of beasts for your strength."

"Not the horns or meat I'm talking about," he mumbled before raising his voice again. "Yes. Female and pure. Unavailable."

"As is our way."

"I'm talking about shield maidens. Must be many who died honorably in battle alongside the males here. The ones I knew were as good as our best!"

"Ah, I see. Yes, many *skaldmaer* were gathered and brought to the halls of the slain here in Asgard."

He ostentatiously turned and surveyed the hall. "I see none."

"Naturally, they are kept separate from the men."

"What?"

"It is our patron goddess' decision. Freya established a different hall, a different practice battlefield. Kept away from the *patriarchy* who would abuse them as was done on Midgard in life."

Patriarchy? What in Odin's name is a patriarchy? Leif grimaced as the meaning came to him. "Yeah, yeah. So how long must we wait for Ragnarök?"

Sigrun glared at him. "It will come when it comes. Then you can sleep forever. Now I have duties." She turned away and headed for her office.

He stared after her. *Well,* he thought, *at least I tried.*

Another thought occurred to him. *So where are they housed?*

Taking one last look around the feasting hall, Leif stepped out into the clean fresh air of Asgard and gazed around. In the distance, beyond the trees and bushes, he made out the rainbow glow of the *Bifröst* bridge, pathway to Midgard. It was as good a place as any to explore his memories of life. He found the track, once well-worn under the feet of the many arrivals: worthy, recently slain warriors. It lay untrodden for centuries and overgrown.

As he ambled toward the glow he made out a human shape in the darkness, sitting on the ground, back resting against a tree, and facing the bridge. *A kindred spirit, maybe?*

A spherical helm unfamiliar to him lay on the ground beside the figure.

He drew nearer and more details became clear. This was no Valkyrie or warrior. It wore a baggy dark green outfit made of a single weave that enclosed the entire body from neck to wrist and ankle.

Perhaps a new arrival. Lost, maybe?

He headed over to offer help, wondering where the guiding Valkyrie was. His feet scuffed the ground. The stranger stood and turned, falling into a defensive crouch, dagger in hand. A silvery stripe ran down from throat to groin. The outfit's chest and upper arms carried strange icons and some meaningless lettering: "Lt. H. Jones."

"Greetings!" Leif called out, drawing nearer and raising his empty right hand. There was no need for caution: he had died many times.

"Oh. Hi!" came the reply as the figure relaxed a little.

He froze. A woman? A woman as tall as Leif himself. A shield maiden, possibly? He took a better look.

She was a *blámaðr,* dark of skin with short curly jet-black hair and eyes as brown as the good earth. One of the folk from the far distant south of his homeland and across the middle sea. He had never been there but tales travel on the wind.

"Er, hello?" Her voice now carried uncertainty.

"Oh, forgive." He continued his slow approach and halted a couple of manslengths away. "Was surprised you were a shieldmaiden. Never met one in Asgard."

She chuckled, her body relaxing more. "And I have never encountered a male warrior. I was told we were kept separate. Our hall is over there. *Maerhalla* it's called." She pointed into the distance.

He looked but saw no buildings.

"I am called Leif." He pointed at her chest. "Is that your name? How do I say it? *Let-ha-yonez?*"

"Helen. Call me Helen." Her smile was warm.

"So what're you doing out here at feasting time?"

She sighed. "I'm vegan. I can't eat most of what they serve and I am tee-total, so no mead."

These were strange words to Leif. *Vegan?* What tribe was that? And *taytotal?* Warriors arriving after Leif spoke of how the world was changing, with new alliances and the rise of a strange new religion from the middle sea. The flow of warriors declined until no new faces feasted at the long table.

The meanings came to him, as they did when early or later arrivals spoke words not used in his years. Something to do with being dead, he guessed. "No meat or alcohol? By Odin, that must be so boring."

She scowled at him and turned away.

Taking a step forward with outstretched hand, he said, "Forgive me. I respect your religion. It is just so foreign to me. But if you are no Odin-worshiper, how came you to Valhalla?"

Helen turned back to face him wearing a frown. "Not a religion, but you're forgiven. My life, my world, must be so different to yours." She paused, looked away, then back at Leif. Taking a deep breath, she asked, "Can I ask, when did you die?"

Leif pushed back his helm and scratched his head. "Not really sure. Maybe a thousand years and so many feasts ago. I stopped counting."

He looked around. Risking the disfavor of the Valkyrie, he added, "The feasts are the same every day. Every day's the same. We wake, we fight, we die, we feast, we sleep. Just hoping Ragnarök arrives soon."

"That's the final battle of the gods and warriors against the frost giants, yes?"

"You don't know?" He blinked and shook his head a little. "That's why we're here. At least why I'm here. So you're not a shield maiden? Why are you here?"

Helen grimaced. "Mistake, I think. I was a fighter pilot. Shot down over–"

The place-name she spoke was meaningless to him. In his time the land was unknown. But *"fighter pilot"* became clear.

"Wait! You fly in the sky and fight? But you're not a Valkyrie?"

"No. Just a pilot. We fly in machines, not by magic."

Leif tried to imagine the wondrous joy at sailing above the clouds, gazing down on the lands and oceans below, sharing the air with the white seabirds, scattering them shrieking as he turned and twisted among them.

"I yearn for knowledge of this. You flew to Asgard in your machine?" he asked.

"Nope. Let me explain. My mother was Danish and taught me all the old stories long ago. I was interested. Just loved the Norse *mythos*. Joined the Air Force, became a pilot. When my plane got hit by a SAM, I cried out 'Odin!' for some reason. A woman swooped from the clouds and carried me here."

He chose not to react as the meaning of *mythos* became clear along with that of *plane*. But, "A *sam*?"

"Surface-to-air missile." Seeing his continuing confusion, she explained, "Like a spear that explodes when it hits you."

He pictured a spear named Sam doing that and took a deep breath. "Where can I get one?" His eagerness bubbled up.

She smiled sympathetically, "Only in Midgard, I'm afraid."

Deflated, he moved on. "So you are a warrior of the air, a great warrior, who did not worship the true gods, but who called out to Odin and the Valkyries heard, finding you worthy. And now here you're in… *Maerhalla*?"

She nodded. "The feasting hall for shield maidens."

"You fight and die every day? Did they give you a flying machine?"

"Nope. I'm learning how to use hand-held weapons.

I'm good with a knife and a pistol – which they won't allow me to use – but the rest..." She looked down and shook her head. "I last about a minute with a dagger against battle axes and longswords, depending on how well I dodge. The Valkyrie are not happy."

"And you hate the feasting. So you came out here for what?"

"To view the Rainbow Bridge and watch for others of my era arriving. I've stood or sat here for over fifty days. For nothing."

"And Maerhalla is full of shield maidens? So where is it again?" His eyebrows rose.

She chuckled. "We're told the hall is hidden from the eyes of men. As is yours to us."

He slumped. "Oh."

"I wonder how things are below. My friends, family, even my country," she said, turning her gaze to the rainbow glow.

He nodded slowly and turned his face away from her to gaze into the distance. "Yes, it's hard at first. It fades with the centuries."

There was a long silence. He repeated, as if trying to convince himself, "It fades."

Without turning his head, Leif said, "After a few decades, everyone I knew was either here or dead on Midgard and gone elsewhere. Family, friends... And as no more arrived from my lands, I guessed the new religion I heard was coming had overcome the old ways. No worshipers any more."

She rested a hand on his shoulder. "Yes. There are no worshipers left. The gods will have to make do with the worthy ones they already have." After a moment she added with bitterness in her voice, "And people like me. People here by accident who have no ancient heavy weapons training."

There was another long silence.

"Tell me of your times, when you lived below," she said.

Settling down beside her, facing the men's combat

field, he spoke awkwardly about his hut, his village, how he lived when on land – the tedious part of life. Soon his gaze drifted to the middle distance as his thoughts wandered across the wilder places beyond his village. He spoke of the great fjords with giant cliffs looming to right and left above the broad river that carried his longship toward the ocean, the estuary opening up into the wide realm of the waters beyond, stretching out into the far distance to lands beyond sight and unknown. He recalled the last backward glance as his homeland grew smaller until barely a thin dark line on the horizon marked his birthing-place, those towering cliffs diminished to insignificance.

He spoke of the voyages across that ocean, whose moods and tempers dominated the warriors who braved those spaces. The joy as the stars needed for navigation emerged in the darkening sky above when the mists dispersed and the clouds flowed away. The gentle rocking of the longship on peaceful waters, turning to dizzying swaying when the storms raged. He told of sails snapping in the winds and hanging loose during the long hours of sweating, backaching strain pulling at the oars when those winds failed, glancing up again and again, seeking the first ruffling of the cloths marking an end to their efforts.

"The wind in my beard, the sea-spray in my face, the first sighting of land, drawing my weapon awaiting the berserker rage that gives me victory…" His voice trailed off.

He calmed, his voice becoming more conversational. "I went west as far as *Snæland* and *Grœnland*, even once all the way to *Vinland*!" He did not hide the braggarting in his voice.

"Vinland? Oh, I visited the dig in Newfoundland and saw the ruins. Amazing!"

"Ruins? His face fell. "The settlement is no more?"

"'Fraid not." She patted his arm and threw him a sympathetic smile. "Everything comes to an end, you know?"

He sighed and looked down at the grass. "Everything? Not this cursed wait for Ragnarök."

"Tell me more. Where else? How about Russia, or the Muslim lands in the south? Your people were fighters and bodyguards there."

"The *Rus* and the strange far south? I know nothing of these places. Farthest south I went was *Jorvik* in *Danelagen* once."

She frowned as the meanings came to her. "The town of York in the Danelaw in England?"

"What? Angle-land? The Anglish drove us out? And the Vinland settlements lie in ruins? What remains of my homeland?" He stared blank-eyed at her. "All gone? Gone to ruins?"

"Oh, it thrives. Democratically and economically. World-leaders."

He sighed. "So the *Ostmen* homeland is a wondrous place, even if the remote settlements were lost? That's some reassurance."

"I know some of the stories, but you grew up with all the beliefs about the end of times. You've been here longer than I have, so you can see any flaws in the legends. Tell me, what really does happen to us after we all die again at Ragnarök?"

"We all die forever. You spoke it, 'everything comes to an end'. No more wakenings and feastings, thank Odin. Though some from a later time say we rise yet again and pass into another realm. A wondrous paradise. More feasting but no more fighting and dying. Some say the idea was stolen from that new religion. What do they say in your time?"

"Oh, I read *online* a scientific theory that the world, the whole universe, is eventually destroyed and the chaos forms a new *Big Bang.*"

The two new concepts in that one sentence set Leif aback. "Online? Big bang? I have no understanding, no references."

"Oh, online is a kind of magic way everyone on Midgard can speak to everyone else. Big Bang is…" She frowned as she spoke slowly, visibly struggling to find words for concepts he would not understand. "Legend tells that the universe was created after the gods defeated the giants. Their king's body was ripped apart and its pieces scattered to form the universe, the realms. In the old tales, after Ragnarök, the world is destroyed, but it will explode forming new realms." She winced her dissatisfaction with her explanation.

"Hmm… I see."

"Then *Líf* and *Lífþrasir* emerge from their place of safety and fill the new world with life." She jerked her head up. "Hey! You're called Leif. Are you *the one*?"

He laughed. "There must be Leifs beyond counting in the halls. Like the one who discovered Snæland." He pondered for a moment. "Although it sounds like a good occupation, surviving beyond the end and breeding like a–" He caught her scowl and fell to silence.

"But," he said, "speaking of which, do the shieldmaidens hunger for menfolk?"

She shrugged. "Some do. Others seem quite pleased with the arrangement."

"Hmm… As in the male halls."

Leif held his tongue while his next question shaped itself. "And how is it with you?"

She looked down. "I miss male company, yes. But I've only been without if it for just fifty days or so, not for your thousand years. I guess it's something that never fades? Just gets worse?" Her eyes lifted to examine his face as he replied.

"Yes." Bitterness rang in his voice.

"I'm sorry."

Silence hung again in the space between them.

"This online you spoke of. Could we use it here to talk to folk below?"

"Nope. Midgard only."

"Oh. I see. Pity."

He considered what he had learned. A female warrior, a pilot, who flew in the skies like the Valkyrie, but in a machine, not by magic. Pilots must avoid exploding spears leaping from the ground. But how did the pilots kill the enemy while traveling high above them?

Pilots did not stand toe-to-toe with the enemy, never saw the anger, hate, and bloodlust in an opponent's eyes, or the fear and dread as their end arrived. Pilots never felt the impact of a longsword against living flesh, never wiped a slain foe's blood-spatter from their eyes, or sheathed a blade as they stood triumphant over an enemy's corpse. These were not warriors as he understood the word but, somehow, this one had proven worthy enough to enter Valhalla. It was not for Leif to judge, though he did.

A great blaring of horns raced across the grass and enveloped them. A thunderous voice shook the ground. "Baldur is dead, killed by Loki. Lament ye all!"

He leapt to his feet. "The first sign! At last! Ragnarök is upon us!"

"What?" She looked up at him and cocked her head.

He snapped at her with a voice bursting with impatience and battle-lust. "The Four Signs. The death of the god Baldur, slain by Loki. The great winter that descends on the realms. The sun and moon disappear. Then Yggdrasil shakes from root to branch, raising the longship *Naglfar* to transport us all to the Ragnarök field to battle and die. Take up your weapons!" His hand fell to the hilt of the sword at his belt as he crouched and scanned his surroundings.

She pursed her lips. "A pistol and a service knife. What good are they against giants who can defeat the gods themselves?"

"We give what we can. In the end, we give our lives," he growled.

"Sounds pretty much like the squadron's motto." She drew both weapons and adopted a combat crouch. "But I don't see any monsters."

"They will come. Out of the great winter's icy darkness, sunless and moonless, they will come."

"But the ship will come transport us to the battlefield?"

Leif thought about it and straightened up. "Hmm...

Yes. Impatience took me. Just been waiting so many centuries for it, for something to happen. Something special."

Something like you, he thought.

A sudden chill wind rose from nowhere, wrapping itself around them, flapping at loose clothing, and ruffling Leif's beard.

"Is this the winter?" she asked as the leaves all around turned golden then russet brown, falling loose, to be swept away by the icy gusts.

A darkness sucked the stars away as the moon's silver glow faded to nothing and the cold intensified.

"But it's so fast. I thought it would take days, weeks, months…" Leif said.

"Everything works faster these days," she said, wrapping her arms around her body, hugging close her body's warmth.

"The wind is coming from the Rainbow Bridge. Get behind the tree!" He had to shout above the strengthening storm.

Together they huddled against the stout trunk. Her shivering grew more intense.

Leif lifted a corner of his fur cloak. "Get under this."

With only a brief pause, she nodded, smiling, and huddled close to him. He wrapped it around her shoulders and held her body close to his.

"Thank you," she mouthed, huddling closer.

By Odin, how many centuries have I longed for a female body pressed against mine. And my wish came true, but not the way I dreamed of.

"You know," she called out above the wind's howling, "I feared you at first, knowing the tales of rapacious Vikings. But you seem to be different."

"Curse those raiders who went a-viking. Everyone thinks we were the same. I was no raider but a guard to traders. Yes, I fought, but against those who would raid the ships or attack the traders on land."

The world darkened further as coal-black clouds filled the sky. Icy rain pelted down, turning the ground beneath their feet to mud. Winds swept wintered leaves around their feet and away into the curtain of falling water that surrounded them. Rain turned to hail, rattling upon their helmets and biting any exposed flesh. They huddled even closer.

Lightning flashed amid the skudding clouds. Earth-shaking thunder roared again and again.

"Odin's summoning his troops. We must get back to the halls. The longship will be coming!"

"I can't see more than a few feet. Can't see the hall."

"We have to try or we won't be there at the final battle."

A dark shape appeared in the veil of hail. Sigrun emerged from the winter's wrath.

"You've come to show us the way!" he thrilled.

"No. You two are unsuited for Ragnarök. You already missed the boat."

"Unsuited? Why? Surely you can take us to the battlefield?"

"You are both too tied to the lives you left behind. Too tied to Midgard. Neither of you settled into the afterlife. You wanted more. You need something else. You need each other. The *Norns* who shape the destinies of humans and even the gods' destinies decreed it."

"So what happens to us?" Helen asked, frowning.

"Follow me." Sigrun turned and strode away.

They obeyed, cloak wrapped around both, struggling against the wind and the mud underfoot.

"Here," Sigrun halted beside Yggdrasil and indicated an opening, a knot-hole, in the vast thickness of the trunk. "Enter."

Dripping wet, the warriors bustled inside the shelter. The storm's raging anger continued outside.

"This place is called *Hoddmimis Holt*. Here are supplies that will last for many days. You will remain here, safe from the battle and weather until the skies clear. You are *Lif*," she nodded at Helen, "and you are *Lifþrasir* of legend," she indicated Leif.

They heard the names from ancient lore, translated now

as "life" and "life's lover and preserver".

"You had it the wrong way around," Sigrun said.

"But I can fight as well as he can, I know it!" Helen folded her arms and stood shivering in defiance.

"Not while heavily pregnant or caring for a newborn. Not with a projectile weapon that can never be reloaded in your lifetime. Protection was this man's trade and protection is his destiny. You must learn to use basic weapons and you will stand beside your mate, warriors together, in protecting their future when biology permits.

"In the world to come, you will produce a new population. You will fill the world with your offspring."

Helen's face fell into astonishment as her eyes opened wide. "Sounds like Adam and Eve."

Sigrun turned to face her, wearing a slight smile. "Old stories share features of truth, no matter how far apart they are in time and space. Most religions mistakenly tell your future as a relic of the past, where two beings – gods or spirits or humans – populate the world. You are actually the ones."

"Seriously?" Leif closed his eyes briefly then glanced at Helen, frowning.

"You wanted a mate," Sigrun reminded him, "and this one is better than any you had before Asgard."

"But... But... She's of Vegan beliefs."

Sigrun chuckled. "You had mead and meat, now you have a maiden mate."

He turned to stare at Helen. "Maiden?"

"Shieldmaiden!" she declared, scowling.

"No meat and no mead?" he moaned.

"Correct." Helen folded her arms as scowl turned to glare.

The storm outside had intensified while they spoke. Sounds of screams and battle cries reached them from far away.

Sigrun sighed, shaking her head a little. "I can see this relationship will require *rather* a lot of work. But now I must return to the field of battle. Freya calls me." She gestured at the sky.

Helen pressed her balled fists against her hips. "You can hold it right there!"

Leif cocked his head and murmured, "I *do* like this one. She has fire."

"What?" Sigrun halted in the act of turning away.

"You expect me to repopulate the whole bloody planet? I'm not a god-damn baby-making machine! And how about ongoing inbreeding, genetic faults, DNA–"

"Hold on." It was Leif's turn to call a halt. Fear hung on his face as he looked down at his body, tapping his fingers against his chest, prodding, probing for something. "Dee-Yen-Eye? I get an image of two entangled snakes inside every part of my body. What is happening?"

"I'll explain later," Helen reassured him, mirth tainting her grim expression. "Looks like we have a lot of time ahead of us."

Sigrun cocked her head. "I don't understand it either but the Norns have decreed it, so it must be right. They have seen inside of you both. You are special, genetically pure for many generations, they say. It will work itself out, do not be afraid."

"So there's no snakes inside me?" Leif asked.

"No." Sigrun grinned reassuringly.

The winds' howlings strengthened. Lightning flashes lit up the sky ever more frequently, casting brief illumination into the wooden cave. Thunder rolled constantly, trembling even the vastness of Yggdrasil.

"But now I really must go. We will never meet again, say the Norns, so enjoy life and each other. Oh, and one last thing. You thought you were waiting for Ragnarök. But Ragnarök was waiting for *you*." Sigrun stepped back into the storm and was gone.

The bedraggled and dripping warriors took a little time, assessing each other in a new light.

Finally, Helen spoke. "Er… Repopulate the world? That's a lot of children…" she said, uncertainly.

"I guess she means we start with a few and they take up the ax, as it were, and continue the task."

"Task?" Helen glared at him, hands on hips, face thrust forward. "You consider intimacy with me a task?"

Bad start, he thought.

The winter endured.

The food supplies lasted.

Leif learned to like vegan food and unfermented fruit juice when shared with Helen.

In time, he also learned the long reflective stripe on her flight suit was a zipper.

She showed him how it worked.

He worked it…

THE END
(Of a new beginning)

ACKNOWLEDGEMENTS

With thanks to Elsewhen Press for their encouragement and support in producing this collection.

A REQUEST

As you've read this far, you probably thought the stories weren't too bad.

Glad to hear it!

So why not post a review and help more people learn about Andy's fiction?

Reviews *really* help an author get known to a wider audience.

Many thanks!

Elsewhen Press

delivering outstanding new talents in speculative fiction

Visit the Elsewhen Press website at elsewhen.press for the latest information on all of our titles, authors and events; to read our blog; find out where to buy our books and ebooks; or to place an order.

Sign up for the Elsewhen Press InFlight Newsletter at elsewhen.press/newsletter

Existence is Elsewhen

Twenty stories from twenty great authors
including
Andy McKell

The title *Existence is Elsewhen* paraphrases the last sentence of André Breton's 1924 *Manifesto of Surrealism*, perfectly summing up the intent behind this anthology of stories from a wonderful collection of authors. Different worlds... different times. It's what Elsewhen Press has been about since we launched our first title in 2011.

Here, we present twenty science fiction stories for you to enjoy. We are delighted that headlining this collection is the fantastic **John Gribbin,** with a worrying vision of medical research in the near future. Future global healthcare is the theme of **J A Christy's** story; while the ultimate in spare part surgery is where **Dave Weaver** takes us. **Edwin Hayward's** search for a renewable protein source turns out to be digital; and **Tanya Reimer's** story with characters we think we know gives us pause for thought about another food we take for granted. Evolution is examined too, with **Andy McKell's** chilling tale of what states could become if genetics are used to drive policy. Similarly, **Robin Moran's** story explores the societal impact of an undesirable evolutionary trend; while **Douglas Thompson** provides a truly surreal warning of an impending disaster that will reverse evolution, with dire consequences.

On a lighter note, we have satire from **Steve Harrison** discovering who really owns the Earth (and why); and **Ira Nayman,** who uses the surreal alternative realities of his *Transdimensional Authority* series as the setting for a detective story mash-up of Agatha Christie and Dashiel Hammett. Pursuing the crime-solving theme, **Peter Wolfe** explores life, and death, on a space station; while **Stefan Jackson** follows a police investigation into some bizarre cold-blooded murders in a cyberpunk future. Going into the past, albeit an 1831 set in the alternate Britain of his *Royal Sorceress* series, **Christopher Nuttall** reports on an investigation into a girl with strange powers.

Strange powers in the present-day is the theme for **Tej Turner,** who tells a poignant tale of how extra-sensory perception makes it easier for a husband to bear his dying wife's last few days. Difficult decisions are the theme of **Chloe Skye's** heart-rending story exploring personal sacrifice. Relationships aren't always so close, as **Susan Oke's** tale demonstrates, when sibling rivalry is taken to the limit. Relationships are the backdrop to **Peter R. Ellis's** story where a spectacular mid-winter event on a newly- colonised distant planet involves a Madonna and Child. Coming right back to Earth and in what feels like an almost imminent future, **Siobhan McVeigh** tells a cautionary tale for anyone thinking of using technology to deflect the blame for their actions. Building on the remarkable setting of Pera from her *LiGa* series, and developing Pera's legendary *Book of Shadow*, **Sanem Ozdural** spins the creation myth of the first light tree in a lyrical and poetic song. Also exploring language, the master of fantastika and absurdism, **Rhys Hughes,** extrapolates the way in which language changes over time, with an entertaining result.

ISBN: 9781908168955 (epub, kindle) / 9781908168856 (320pp paperback)
Visit bit.ly/ExistenceIsElsewhen

ABOUT THE AUTHOR

author |ˈɔːθə|
noun
>   Someone who tells lies about things that didn't happen to people who don't exist.

Andy was abducted by science fiction pulp magazines and fell in love with classic noir in his early teens. He worked in marketing, franchising, and computing in London and Luxembourg before launching his own web design company. In 2011, he sold the company and retired early to write, act, and travel.

His multi-genre short stories have appeared in various anthologies, he continues to develop science fiction novels, and has branched-out into classic noir.

He has little time for acting, these days.

He hopes you enjoy reading the adventures of his imaginary friends.

You can find out more about Andy on his Blog, follow him on social media, and sign up for his newsletter for updates, background info and promotions:

http://andymckell.com/bibliography
http://andymckell.com   (Blog)
http://bit.ly/AndySignUp   (Newsletter)
https://www.facebook.com/AndyMcKell.Author/